Praise for

High Marks for Murder

"Wonderful storytelling . . . A superb ghost story."
—Emily Brightwell

"An enjoyable mystery set in England's dynamic Edwardian period that is sure to please . . . The characters are intriguing, each with a hint of a tragic past."
—*The Romance Readers Connection*

"Very well done and definitely for those who like their mysteries on the lighter side." —ReviewingTheEvidence.com

"School headmistress Meredith Llewellyn is bright and intuitive and the paranormal atmosphere adds an interesting touch."
—*Romantic Times*

"Very atmospheric [with] a gothic feel . . . Readers will give high marks to Ms. Kent for an interesting, creative whodunit."
—*Genre Go Round Reviews*

"A great cozy writer."
—*Gumshoe Review*

D0450908

MURDER
HAS NO CLASS

Rebecca Kent

BERKLEY PRIME CRIME, NEW YORK

THE BERKLEY PUBLISHING GROUP
Published by the Penguin Group
Penguin Group (USA) Inc.
375 Hudson Street, New York, New York 10014, USA
Penguin Group (Canada), 90 Eglinton Avenue East, Suite 700, Toronto, Ontario M4P 2Y3, Canada
(a division of Pearson Penguin Canada Inc.)
Penguin Books Ltd., 80 Strand, London WC2R 0RL, England
Penguin Group Ireland, 25 St. Stephen's Green, Dublin 2, Ireland (a division of Penguin Books Ltd.)
Penguin Group (Australia), 250 Camberwell Road, Camberwell, Victoria 3124, Australia
(a division of Pearson Australia Group Pty. Ltd.)
Penguin Books India Pvt. Ltd., 11 Community Centre, Panchsheel Park, New Delhi—110 017, India
Penguin Group (NZ), 67 Apollo Drive, Rosedale, North Shore 0632, New Zealand
(a division of Pearson New Zealand Ltd.)
Penguin Books (South Africa) (Pty.) Ltd., 24 Sturdee Avenue, Rosebank, Johannesburg 2196,
South Africa

Penguin Books Ltd., Registered Offices: 80 Strand, London WC2R 0RL, England

This is a work of fiction. Names, characters, places, and incidents either are the product of the author's imagination or are used fictitiously, and any resemblance to actual persons, living or dead, business establishments, events, or locales is entirely coincidental. The publisher does not have any control over and does not assume any responsibility for author or third-party websites or their content.

MURDER HAS NO CLASS

A Berkley Prime Crime Book / published by arrangement with the author

PRINTING HISTORY
Berkley Prime Crime mass-market edition / January 2010

Copyright © 2010 by Doreen Roberts Hight.
Cover illustration by Griesback/Martucci.
Cover design by George Long.
Interior text design by Kristin del Rosario.

ISBN: 978-0-425-23207-1

BERKLEY® PRIME CRIME
Berkley Prime Crime Books are published by The Berkley Publishing Group,
a division of Penguin Group (USA) Inc.,
375 Hudson Street, New York, New York 10014.
BERKLEY® PRIME CRIME and the PRIME CRIME logo are trademarks of Penguin Group (USA) Inc.

PRINTED IN THE UNITED STATES OF AMERICA

10 9 8 7 6 5 4 3 2 1

To Bill, for always believing in me, no matter what I do.

Acknowledgments

Sadly, this is the final book in the series. I enjoyed writing about the adventures of Meredith, Felicity, and Essie, and I shall miss them. I do want to thank the people who helped me bring to life the students and staff of the Bellehaven Finishing School for Young Ladies.

My astute editor, Sandra Harding, whose eagle eye and shrewd comments saved me from making too many blunders.

My energetic agent, Paige Wheeler, whose enthusiasm and support keep me motivated and busy.

Berkley's brilliant art department, who are so good at transforming my words into a charming, intricate scene on the cover.

My loyal fans, for all the wonderful e-mails and letters. Thank you so much for taking the time to write to me. You make my day.

My husband, Bill. For all that you do and all that you are.

Chapter 1

Meredith Llewellyn stepped briskly across the courtyard, her brow furrowed and her lips compressed. If there was one thing she hated, it was starting out the day with a confrontation. There were times when her responsibilities as headmistress of the Bellehaven Finishing School could become quite irksome.

Usually she enjoyed her morning walk in the grounds before classes began. Early spring was her favorite time of the year, when daffodils poked green shoots through the dark earth and the heady scent of lavender was just a delightful promise away.

The flower gardens lining the lawns of the Bellehaven Finishing School for Young Ladies had begun to stir once more. Birds trilled among the thickening leaves of the poplars, and sunshine brightened the gray walls of the ancient school building. That was the beauty of spring, full of hope and promise.

Not that Meredith spent much time on wishful thinking. Just a few short years into the new century, already the world was changing at an alarming rate. New inventions seemed to pop up everywhere and it had become quite a challenge to keep pace with everything going on.

At Bellehaven however, the emphasis was more on teaching young women how to take their proper place in their future lives.

Meredith loved teaching fine arts to her students, adored her fellow tutors—well, two of them, at least. The third, Sylvia Montrose, could be somewhat of a problem at times, but Meredith was adept at turning awkward situations into something a little less hazardous.

She reached the steps leading to the front doors of the school and hurried up them. All said, she reminded herself, life was good for the most part, and if she had a couple of thorns in her side to contend with, well, that was a small price to pay.

It was one of those thorns, however, that had spoiled her morning stroll, and she couldn't help feeling just a little resentful. The sooner she dealt with the source of her irritation, the better.

A babble of voices greeted her as she entered the lobby, and at the sight of her, the group of students quickly dispersed. Any minute now the bell would ring for the first class, and Meredith had established a strict policy for punctuality. Discipline had to be maintained at all costs—not an easy task with fifty spirited and often rebellious young ladies taking up occupancy in the hallowed halls of Bellehaven.

Frowning now, Meredith marched down the corridor to her office. She was not looking forward to the impending meeting with her assistant, Roger Platt. The young man had a roguish eye for the girls, and an unfortunate penchant for stirring up trouble.

More than once Meredith had come close to dismissing the unrepentant assistant. She had complained, often with a certain amount of vehemence to Stuart Hamilton, who had hired the rascal. Upon each occasion the disturbingly handsome owner of Bellehaven had persuaded her to give the assistant another chance and, much to her chagrin, she had capitulated, albeit with a certain amount of resentment.

Yes, Meredith thought, as she twisted the handle of the door and threw it open, Roger Platt was a definite thorn in her side, and only slightly more so than the annoying Stuart Hamilton.

The young man in question lifted his head as Meredith entered the room, then sprang to his feet, managing to knock over the ink bottle, which mercifully, was still capped. "Good m-morning, Mrs. Llewellyn." He righted the bottle, began to sit down again, corrected himself and lunged out from behind her desk. "You'll be needing your desk, I assume. I'll take these accounts to the library and—"

Meredith halted him with a shake of her head. "No need, I'm on my way to the classroom. I just stopped by to ask you about an incident in the art studio last night."

Roger's face turned dark red. Using his thumb, he carefully removed a lock of dark brown hair from over his eye. "Art s-studio?"

"Yes, Mr. Platt. It has come to my attention that you and one of my students were seen leaving there at an indecent hour, and I should like an explanation."

The young man looked right and then left, as if seeking an escape. Finding none, he stared down at his feet, then switched his gaze to the window. "I was—ah—helping the young lady look for a lost sketch book."

"A lost sketch book." She was happy to see Roger wince at the heavy skepticism in her voice.

"Ah . . . yes. I was on my way out when Sophie . . . I mean . . . Miss Westchester, caught up with me in the corridor and requested my help."

"Miss Westchester couldn't look for a sketch book by herself?"

Roger poked a finger inside his starched shirt collar as if it had become too tight. "She . . . ah . . . was afraid to go in there in the dark. I fetched an oil lamp and held it for her while she looked for the book."

Meredith narrowed her eyes and reminded herself that as a lady and a representative of authority it was imperative to hold her temper. "May I ask what you were doing in the building at that late hour? Your duties are supposed to be completed by seven o'clock."

Roger nodded, his gaze flicking across her face, presumably to gauge her reaction to his tale. "I had trouble balancing the ledgers and had stayed late to finish them." He tried a wobbly smile. "I thought that's what you would want me to do."

Aware that she was losing this particular battle only intensified Meredith's frustration. She was certain that Roger Platt had been engaging in indiscreet behavior with Sophie Westchester, who was no angel herself.

Meredith was just as convinced that Roger knew that she knew, and was congratulating himself on having evaded a reprimand. Nevertheless, she could hardly accuse the young man of lying without some kind of evidence.

Eying him with as much menace as possible, she leaned forward to emphasize her unspoken warning. "I assume the lady in question will confirm your story?"

To her annoyance, Roger smiled with a little more enthusiasm. "I'm quite sure she will, Mrs. Llewellyn."

About to inform him of the consequences should he be lying, she opened her mouth to speak. At that moment, however, something in the corner of the room caught her attention. Over by the filing cabinet she could see something glowing.

For a shocked moment she thought something was on fire as the misty patch of light deepened to a bright red, then flickered and faded to a pale pink. Just as she was about to point it out to Roger, it gradually dwindled away, leaving only the dark shadows in the corner of the room.

Shaken, Meredith stared at the empty space for several moments, until Roger's sharp voice jerked her back.

"Is something wrong?" He turned his head to follow her gaze, his face registering confusion.

"No, of course not." She backed away, one hand reaching for the door. "I thought I saw a mouse, that's all. I'll have to ask the maintenance man to set a trap. Reggie Tupper is very good at trapping mice."

"A cat," Roger announced, sounding insufferably smug.

"I beg your pardon?"

"A cat, that's what you need. That's what will get rid of them. We had three cats in the orphanage where I grew up. Overrun with mice there, we were."

"Oh, dear." Meredith's hand touched the door and she grabbed the edge of it for support. "Yes, well, carry on, Mr. Platt. I will need all those accounts reconciled by this afternoon."

"Yes, m'm." Roger nodded and smiled, his brown eyes simmering with relief.

Meredith stepped out into the hallway and snapped the

door shut with a little more force than she'd intended. Taking a deep breath, she focused on recovering her composure.

Her mind playing tricks, that's all it was. Just because she'd been visited by a couple of ghosts in the past, it didn't mean—it *couldn't* mean—yet another apparition was hovering nearby, waiting to seek her help. It had been five months since the last encounter. She had just about convinced herself that her strange and unpredictable ability to see and communicate with departed beings was no longer in demand.

Giving herself a mental shake, she hurried down the hallway to her classroom. There was no time to worry about it now. She had twelve young ladies to instruct in the art of clay sculpture and she simply could not waste her precious time on what could well be a figment of her imagination.

Grace Parker picked up a fork and examined it with a critical eye. "This one's got egg on it," she announced. "You didn't wash it properly."

Standing at the sink, Olivia Bunting grunted. "Just go ahead and polish it. No one will ever notice."

"Mrs. Wilkins will notice."

"No, she won't. We'll have it out on the tables in the dining room before she gets back."

Grace spat on the fork and rubbed it with a corner of her apron. "Where is she, anyhow?"

"She's upstairs in Mona Fingle's office, going over the weekly menus." Olivia lifted a pile of silverware out of the soapy water and dumped it on the draining board. "I don't know why she bothers. What the heck does Mona know about cooking, anyway?"

"Well, she *is* the housekeeper, after all. It's her job to decide what to put on the menus."

"Yeah, but Wilky's the cook, and she knows what the girls like to eat."

Grace examined the fork once more, then smeared silver polish over the egg-stained prongs. "And all we are is the housemaids, so we have to mind our own blinking business, don't we."

Olivia spun around, one dripping hand tucking stray dark hairs under her cap. "Gawd, hark at you. We're not just housemaids, we're suffragettes, so there."

Grace laid the fork on the tray next to its gleaming companions and picked up another one from the pile waiting to be polished. "Fat lot of good that does us. We get into trouble every time we get anywhere near them suffragettes. Look what happened when we went to that protest with Christabel Pankhurst. You almost got thrown into prison and I had to come and rescue you."

Olivia grinned. "Yeah, that was a lot of fun."

"Fun?" Grace shook the fork at her. "It wouldn't have been so much fun if you'd been shoved in prison."

Turning back to the sink, Olivia shrugged. "Well, I didn't get shoved into prison, so there's no need to get all stirred up about it, is there."

Grace sighed. Sometimes she wondered why she paid attention to Olivia and her wild ideas. So far they'd been lucky, and although they had come close to being sacked by Mona, Mrs. Wilkins had come to their rescue and saved their jobs. Though they'd given up far too many of their precious days off as punishment for their escapades.

"Anyhow," Olivia said, her voice muffled by the clinking of silverware in the sink, "this time I've got a better idea."

Grace felt a pang of dismay. "Not again. After the last time I told you I wasn't going on any more protests."

Olivia dropped the last pile of wet silverware on the draining board, and wiped her hands on her apron. "The reason we got into trouble before was because we were with the WSPU. There was a lot of suffragettes there so they got a lot of attention from the bobbies."

"I thought that was the idea."

Olivia shook her head, dislodging her hair once more. She shoved it back with an impatient hand. "Well, I know that, but what if we organized our own protest, on a much smaller scale? We'd still be doing our part for the women's movement, and if we do it in the village instead of in Witcheston, there'll only be one bobby to stop us."

Grace looked at her in horror. "A protest in Crickling Green? You must be mad. Everyone in the village knows us."

"They won't see us in the crowd."

"What crowd? Where are we going to get a crowd of suffragettes who'll come to the village to protest? Besides, I thought you said you didn't want to use the WSPU."

"I don't." Olivia looked awfully pleased with herself. "We'll get *our* girls to do it with us."

For a long moment Grace stared at her. "*Our* girls?"

Olivia nodded. "The students of Bellehaven."

"Now I know you've gone bonkers."

"Why?"

"For one thing, they won't do it."

"Course they will. They'll do anything for a bit of excitement."

"Well, if they do, they could be expelled."

"Nah." Olivia picked up the silverware from the draining board and carried it across the kitchen to the table.

"They would have to catch us first, and like I said, there's only one bobby in Crickling Green and he's not too swift in the head."

"P.C. Shipham can be really nasty when he's cross."

"Yeah, well, like I said, he's got to catch us first."

Grace fought back a sense of panic. This was a bad idea, she could feel it in her bones. She knew Olivia, though. Once her friend made up her mind there was no changing it.

As if reading her thoughts, Olivia fixed her with a determined stare. "You're not going to let me down now, are you?"

Grace slowly shook her head. Olivia was not only her best friend, she was her only friend. That relationship rested on Olivia's expectations of complete and unconditional loyalty. Do what Olivia wanted, or bugger off.

As always, Grace chose the friendship over good sense. "No," she said, with a quiver of apprehension, "but I don't have to like it."

"Oh, come on, don't be such a scaredy-cat. It's going to be fun."

Grace had to wonder how many more days off she'd lose to Olivia's idea of fun. "Where are we going to hold the protest? We don't have no town hall in the village."

"No, but we have a pub." Olivia's smile was triumphant. "Just think about it. All those old geezers sipping beer in the public bar, telling us we're not allowed in there. Blinking nerve of 'em. Who are they to tell us where we can and can't go?" She flung out an arm in a dramatic gesture of defiance. "We'll show 'em. I can just see their faces when we all march in there." She started pumping her arm up and down. "We want the vote! We want the vote! Equal rights for women! We want the vote!"

Grace stared down at the fork in her hand. Disaster. That's what this latest daft idea would bring. She could feel it in her bones.

All through her instruction that morning Meredith found herself glancing into the corners of the room, half expecting to see the red glow appear again. When the bell rang for the end of morning class with nothing untoward happening, she breathed a sigh of relief. She must have imagined it after all. No doubt brought on by the stress of Roger Platt's unquenchable thirst for inappropriate female companionship.

The midday meal, as always, was a noisy affair. Each of the four tutors sat at the head of the long dining tables attempting to keep order, which was often a thankless and fruitless task. Many of Bellehaven's pupils were headstrong, displaying a firm preference for the activities of militant suffragettes instead of learning how to conduct themselves with proper decorum.

Felicity Cross, the spirited, outspoken tutor of languages and literature, always with a heavy dash of modern day politics thrown in, had raised her voice and could be heard above the din admonishing her rowdy students with dire threats and warnings, most of which were blithely ignored.

Esmeralda Pickard, on the other hand, fair of face and delicate as a newly formed rose, seemed to have her students mesmerized as she addressed them in her soft voice. Essie, as everyone called her, was a firm believer in teaching by example.

Do as I say and as I do, was her motto.

The youngest of the tutors, and not too intellectual by

academic standards, she had grown up in an elite environment and was well equipped to instruct the young ladies in the finer points of etiquette and social behavior. Being the closest in age to the young women in her charge, she enjoyed an affiliation with her students not shared by the other tutors.

The fourth tutor and home management expert, Sylvia Montrose, had been handpicked by Stuart Hamilton, and had immediately drawn battle lines between herself and Felicity. The language teacher, in Sylvia's biased opinion, was contributing to the delinquency of her pupils by encouraging them to follow the dictates of the Women's Social and Political Union, instead of teaching them how to become refined, dutiful wives, successful socialites, and a credit to their future husbands.

Meredith did not care for Sylvia's methods or her attitude. She refused to admit, even to herself, that her disapproval might just be due to a touch of jealousy. Sylvia's strawberry blond hair, green eyes, and girlish figure certainly seemed to capture Stuart Hamilton's attention. Not, of course, that it mattered to Meredith one whit upon whom the owner lavished his regard.

Today, however, she was not thinking about Stuart Hamilton or his misguided affections. The memory of the red glow kept popping into her mind, and now she couldn't wait until she could adjourn to the teacher's lounge and share her concerns with her two best friends.

Chapter 2

The long mealtime eventually came to an end. With a sense of urgency now, Meredith dismissed the girls at her table and followed them out into the corridor. Felicity was several steps ahead of her, and paused to allow her to catch up.

"What bee have you got in your bonnet today?" she demanded, her rasping voice carrying down the hallway as always. "I could see the lines in your forehead from across the room."

Meredith shook her head. "Not now. Let's wait until we are in the lounge."

Felicity's eyes lit up. "Something juicy?"

Meredith had to smile. "You are incorrigible, Felicity. Always thinking the worst."

Her comment drew a grin from her friend. "That's the only kind of news that's exciting."

Raised voices farther down the corridor wiped Felicity's grin from her face. Striding forward, she reached a group of students, two of whom were waving arms and spitting words at each other.

"Enough!" Felicity's roar reduced all chattering in the hallways to silence. The two who were arguing glowered at each other, but remained silent while Felicity demanded to know what the disagreement was about.

One of the bystanders decided to be helpful. "They were fighting over a boyfriend," she announced, just as Meredith reached the group.

Felicity's face grew dark. "No one in this school has a boyfriend," she roared. "Boyfriends are nasty, lecherous beings whose only aim is to bring you heartache and disgrace. They are to be avoided at all costs. Is that clear?"

Both girls nodded, though not with too much conviction.

Recognizing one of the contenders, Meredith pinched her lips. She had no doubt about whom Sophie Westchester had been quarreling. As the students hurried off, Meredith beckoned to the young woman and drew her aside. "I understand you were in the art studio late last night," she said, without preamble.

Sophie immediately shot a desperate look after her departing friends, then stared down at the floor. "Yes, miss," she mumbled.

"I am also led to believe that someone else was in there with you."

Sophie's cheeks turned pink. "Er—yes, miss. It was Mr. Platt."

"May I ask what you were doing in the art studio with Mr. Platt at that late hour?"

Sophie poked the toe of her shoe out from under her skirt and stared at it as if she'd never seen it before. "Looking for my palette?"

She'd phrased the answer as a question and Meredith tightened her lips. "Mr. Platt seemed to think you were looking for a sketch book."

"Oh, that's right. My sketch book. I forgot."

Meredith curled her fingers into her palms. "I suggest, Miss Westchester, that the next time you search for a missing article late at night, you do so alone. Otherwise I shall feel strongly compelled to inform your parents of your unfortunate behavior."

"Yes, Mrs. Llewellyn."

"You may leave."

"Yes, miss." Dipping her head, Sophie backed away, then turned and fled down the hallway after her friends.

Staring after her, Meredith frowned. One more strike against the unprincipled Mr. Platt. Something would have to be done about that young man, and soon.

Essie was already seated by the fire when Meredith followed Felicity into the teacher's lounge. She smiled as the women entered the room. "I was wondering what kept you both."

Felicity grunted. "Idiotic girls. Arguing over some young wastrel. What a stupendous waste of time."

Essie raised her eyebrows at Meredith, who shook her head. Felicity's apparent hatred of the male species was legendary. "It was nothing. I took care of it." She glanced over at the empty chairs. "Sylvia hasn't arrived yet."

"With any luck she'll have something pressing to take care of and leave us in peace." Felicity threw herself down on her chair. "Lord, these shoes will be the death of me." She frowned at the offending black Oxfords sticking out from under her long skirt. "I swear I'm getting gout or something."

"It's because they are new." Essie poked a dainty

foot out from under her frock. "These hurt me when I first started wearing them, but now they are quite comfortable."

"I don't see how," Felicity murmured. "All those straps digging into your foot. Give me a sensible lace-up anytime."

Meredith drew a deep breath. "I saw a red glow in my office this morning!"

Two faces turned to stare at her in astonishment.

Meredith gave them both a weak smile. She hadn't meant to blurt it out like that, but any minute Sylvia Montrose could stroll in and her opportunity to discuss the matter with her friends would be lost.

She needed that reassurance from them, to free her mind from worry in order to conduct her classes that afternoon with any degree of competence.

"A red glow?" Essie looked confused. "Do you mean the sunrise?"

"I think she means something else," Felicity murmured. "Were you thinking it was another ghost, perhaps?"

Essie gasped, her eyes growing wide. "Oh, no, Meredith. I thought you were finished with all that."

"So did I." Meredith leaned over and retrieved her knitting bag from the small cabinet at her side. Holding knitting needles helped to steady her hands whenever she was out of sorts.

"Are you sure it was a ghost?"

Felicity had sounded skeptical as usual. Meredith sighed. "No, I'm not. In fact, I'm not even sure now that I actually saw a glow. I was having a rather tense conversation with Roger Platt at the time and may well have imagined the whole thing. I merely wanted to mention it so I could perhaps put the entire incident out of my mind."

"It could have been a trick of the light," Essie said, looking anxious.

"Or your eyes deceiving you." Felicity leaned forward. "Perhaps you need them examined. You may need to wear spectacles. After all, staring all day at those atrocious paintings your students produce must have an adverse effect on your eyes."

Meredith tried to curb her resentment. Felicity was well known for her sharp tongue and rarely meant her words in the way they were presented. Still, she couldn't help getting just a little defensive. "My students do quite well considering they are not accomplished artists."

"Oh, bosh, Meredith, don't take offense." Felicity passed a weary hand over her forehead. "You know I wasn't casting aspersions on your ability to teach. It's the student's fault if she's unable to share your visions and produce them adequately on the page."

"Well, perhaps I should pay a visit to the opticians." Meredith drew out a length of knitting from the bag and laid it in her lap. "Much as I detest the idea of wearing spectacles, it is far better than having to deal with another ghost."

"The last one almost killed you," Essie said, her voice fearful.

"Considering she was supposedly just a child, her presence really did seem to cause a lot of trouble for everyone." Felicity leaned down to rub at the toe of her shoe.

"It wasn't her fault." Meredith grasped the needles in her lap and examined the stitches clinging to one of them. "She asked for my help. How could I deny a child whose life had been so tragically shortened, not to mention those of her entire family? I had to find out who was responsible."

"Well, you can certainly deny this one." Felicity sat up again. "Though I must say I'm inclined to believe your vision was more likely attributed to your eyesight than a visit from the other side."

"I hope you're right." Meredith looked up as the door opened and Sylvia walked in. For now, the discussion was over, but she had an uncomfortable feeling that the matter was far from resolved. Much as she wanted to believe she had imagined that glow in the corner, she couldn't ignore the possibility that once more a ghost was hovering within her vicinity, just waiting for the opportunity to beg her assistance.

"If Mona finds out what we're up to she'll send us both packing." Grace dragged the carpet sweeper behind her, bumping it on every stair on the way up. "You know we're not supposed to mix with the students."

"We do a lot of things we're not supposed to do." Olivia stood at the top of the stairs, a bucket in one hand and a mop in the other. "All we've got to do is sneak into the library after they get out of class. There'll be plenty of girls in there then. We'll tell just a few what we're doing, and hope they tell their friends."

Grace's eyebrows shot up in alarm. "*Wot*? Are you off your rocker? What if the teachers hear about it?"

"We'll swear everyone to secrecy. We'll tell them that if the teachers find out, the whole thing will be off. What's more, if someone tells on us, we'll find out who it is and make her wish she'd kept her blinking mouth shut."

Grace shivered. "I don't like this, Olivia. I really don't. It's not worth it. We could really lose our jobs if we get into trouble again."

"We won't lose our jobs." The bucket clanged in Olivia's hand as she swung around and started down the corridor. "Where are they going to get two hard workers like us in Crickling Green? All the young girls are going up to the city to go into service there. Nobody wants to work in this godforsaken place. There's nowhere to go, nothing to do, and only a bunch of louts in the village."

"Why do you stay then?"

Olivia dumped the bucket on the floor and looked at her. "Sometimes I ask myself that same question. I don't know. Maybe it's because I know you won't go to the city with me and I can't leave you here all alone."

Grace felt tears filling her eyes. When Olivia talked like that she'd walk barefoot on burning coals for her. "When are we going to do the protest then?"

Olivia grinned. "On Saturday. It's the first of May. May Day. They'll be dancing around the maypole on the village green that day, and old fish-face Shipham will be watching over them all. He'll be too busy to pay attention to what's going on at the Dog and Duck, and by the time he realizes something's up, we'll be long gone."

Still not convinced, Grace tried to look enthusiastic. "Good. You've got it all worked out, then."

"You bet I have, and don't worry, Grace." Olivia picked up the bucket again. "There's only a bunch of old geezers what goes into the pub midday. We'll march through the public bar, smash all the glasses we can get our hands on and we'll be out of there before they can struggle out of their chairs."

Grace felt her jaw drop. "Smash the glasses?"

Olivia turned her back on her. "Well, of course. What's the use of protesting if you don't do a little damage on the way?"

Prison, that's where they were going to end up, Grace was sure of it. Still, even prison with Olivia was better than life without her. Shoving the sweeper in front of her, Grace started pushing it back and forth across the carpet. All she had to do was remember what her friend had said about not leaving her alone. That gave her the courage she needed. Votes for women. It was a good cause. Maybe Olivia was right. Maybe this time it would all turn out all right.

Standing in front of a dozen or so expectant pupils, Meredith raised her hand. "We will take that again from the second chorus. On the count of three. One, two, three!" She began conducting, and the voices soared in harmony.

At least, they were supposed to harmonize. The actual sound that erupted from the throats of the earnest young students more closely resembled a crowd of unruly onlookers at a hockey match than a finely tuned choral group. Bach was no doubt turning over in his grave.

Frowning, Meredith turned to the piano and played the opening notes of the chorus, singing along with great emphasis to illustrate the harmony. "Now, do you hear that?" She played and sang it again for good measure. "Now that's what I want to hear."

She was about to turn back when something moved into her vision. Her hands froze on the keys as she stared at the red glow hovering near the center of the room. It seemed to billow up from the ground like smoke, weaving and swaying as if caught by the wind.

She blinked, twice, but the mist remained, thickening now. The edges of it were dark red, and the center swirled in angry coils of scarlet and pink.

Aware of the uneasy silence behind her, Meredith leaned forward over the piano and whispered hoarsely, "Go away! Leave me alone!"

The silence was broken by whispers and a muffled giggle. At the sound, the mist seemed to curl in on itself, and then it vanished.

Meredith lifted trembling hands from the keys, pausing for a long moment to steady herself. Behind her, the students shuffled feet, softly coughed, and whispered among themselves.

Turning, Meredith cleared her throat. "All right," she said firmly. "From the second chorus. One, two, three."

The result was not much better, but at least she had managed to regain their attention. There was not a single doubt in her mind that she had been the only one to see the red mist. She had discovered early on that no one else could see her visions—or whatever they were. Most of the time she could barely see them herself.

Whatever ability she possessed to communicate with the dead was limited at best. So far she had not been able to converse with the ghosts, and could only see them for short intervals at a time.

Since they seemed intent on her solving some kind of mystery concerning their deaths, that made things somewhat complicated. She had learned that the only way the ghosts would leave was if she was successful in finding out the truth about their demise, and the only help she got from them were vague clues rendered by little more than gestures and pointing at various objects. All very frustrating, to say the least.

Now, it seemed, she was about to be visited by yet another ghost looking for justice. It was not a task she anticipated with any pleasure.

Thankful when at last she could dismiss the class, Meredith headed for the teacher's lounge. Felicity and Essie had helped her in the past, though with obvious reluctance. Felicity refused to express any belief in ghosts, and no doubt suspected Meredith of investigating the previous murders simply on a whim, while Essie was scared to death of the apparitions, despite the fact she couldn't see them.

Nevertheless, Meredith was determined to get her friends involved right from the start. Three heads were better than one. With their help she might possibly solve whatever mystery awaited her in short order and be rid of the annoying inconvenience of being haunted by a less than constructive wraith with an ax to grind.

She was halfway down the hallway when a deep, masculine voice spoke her name. "Meredith! I hoped to catch you in between your classes. It seems I am in luck."

Inwardly cursing her unfortunate timing, she slowed her steps and came to a halt. Approaching her at a rapid pace was Stuart Hamilton, his face wreathed in a smile.

Dealing with Bellehaven's charming owner was difficult for Meredith at the best of times. She had no idea why, but the man had a way of putting her off guard. Whenever in his presence, she found herself unable to think clearly and inevitably ended up saying or doing something foolish. For days afterward she would cringe at the memory.

Today was definitely not the best of times. She was still unnerved by the vision of the red mist, wondering what was in store for her this time. What she didn't need right now was Hamilton confusing her even more.

Chapter 3

Meredith had trouble summoning an answering smile as the imposing owner reached her. "Mr. Hamilton. I had no idea that you were expected today."

His smile faded. "I rather hoped that we were on first name terms, Meredith. Could you not find it in your heart to call me Stuart?"

His dark eyes rested on her face, confusing her further. He had used her first name for the first time a few months earlier, and she had yet to find the daring to return the compliment. As long as he remained Mr. Hamilton, she could keep a professional distance between them. For some reason, that seemed desperately important.

She covered her confusion by saying briskly, "Was there something you needed to discuss with me?"

He answered with a sigh. "I just wanted to give you a word of caution. Crickling Green is about to be invaded by a very large group of men, most of them young and virile, from what I've heard. The Dog and Duck has been chosen as a location for the national darts championship, and one of the preliminary contests will be held there. I thought, given the nature of young men when in the presence of gullible young ladies, particularly when said young men have been imbibing ale or spirits, that it might be prudent to keep an eye on your students while the contestants are in the village."

Meredith let out a puff of breath. Wonderful. Exactly what she needed on top of everything else. "I'll do my best. Though I'm sure you're aware that it isn't always possible to safeguard fifty vigorous young women. Particularly when they don't want to be protected. Can nothing be done to change the location of the darts match?"

"I'm afraid not. There's no time. The contest is to be held this Saturday, the first of May. Unfortunately I didn't get word of it until this morning."

"I see. Well, we shall simply have to do the best we can."

She hesitated, then added, "As long as I have your attention, there is something else I would like to mention." She glanced up and down the corridor to make sure they were alone.

"Madam, you always have my undivided and most riveted attention."

Certain he was being facetious, she glanced up at him. Not only was his expression solemn, his eyes conveyed a sincerity that caused her heart to beat at an uncomfortable rate. Flustered, she placed a hand at her breast, then as his gaze followed the movement, hastily lowered it again. "I appreciate that, Mr. Hamilton."

"Stuart."

"Yes, well, the matter I wish to discuss with you concerns Mr. Platt."

Hamilton sighed, and rolled his eyes heavenward. "What has he done now?"

"He has engaged in nefarious behavior with one of my students again."

One of Hamilton's eyebrows raised and he pursed his lips. It was a habit that invariably rattled Meredith's composure and today was no exception. Dragging her gaze away from his mouth, she added primly, "I really do think we need to discuss a replacement for that young man. After all, I—"

"What kind of nefarious behavior?"

She snapped her mouth shut and swallowed. "I beg your pardon?"

"I asked what kind of behavior has Mr. Platt conducted to earn such outrage?"

"What kind?"

"Yes." Hamilton leaned forward until his face was much too close to hers. Drawing out his words, he murmured, "What . . . has . . . he . . . done . . . exactly?"

She searched her mind for words. "Well . . . ah . . . he was seen leaving the art studio with the student at an extremely late hour."

"How late?"

She was beginning to get annoyed. Who was he to question her judgment? After all, she was in charge of Bellehaven, not he. What did he know about managing a school of this nature? "I am not aware of the exact hour, Mr. Hamilton, but I can assure you it was well after the student was supposed to have retired to her room, and several hours after Mr. Platt's duties for the day were completed."

"I see." He tucked his thumbs into his waistcoat pockets and rocked back on his heels. "What exactly were they doing in the art room?"

Meredith set her jaw. "I can only imagine."

"But you don't know for certain."

"Their stories were conflicting."

"Ah, so you did question them."

"Indeed I did."

"Then I'm afraid we shall just have to take their word for it." He smiled. "Come, Meredith, I doubt any real harm was done. I'll have a word with Pratt—"

"His name is Platt," Meredith reminded him. Not that it would make any difference. For some reason Stuart Hamilton insisted on calling the assistant Pratt, and no amount of correcting and reminding seemed to penetrate.

"—and warn him of the consequences should the incident be repeated."

"I have warned him many times already." She made herself look directly into Hamilton's face. "I really don't understand why you are so lenient with him. The young man is willful and quite immoral and I consider him a danger to the welfare of my students."

"Don't you think you are being somewhat harsh?"

A gleam had appeared in Hamilton's eyes that warned her she was treading on dangerous ground. She pinched her lips, then muttered, "All I have to say to that, Mr. Hamilton, is that you will have to deal with the consequences should your ward damage the reputation of any of my students."

"May I remind you, Mrs. Llewellyn, that it takes two to two-step." He gave her a stiff bow, then turned sharply on his heel and strode away down the corridor.

Miserably she stared after him. The ache under her ribs was out of proportion, and should have been overwhelmed by the indignation of having her authority usurped in such an arrogant matter. Yet right at that moment what mattered to her most was that Stuart Hamilton had reverted to using her last name again. How very immature of her.

As she expected, Felicity and Essie received the news of her second vision of the red mist with completely opposite reactions. Felicity urged her to have Reggie check all the gas lamps in the building, while Essie begged her to turn her back on the ghost and refuse to help.

It was with some trepidation that Meredith retired to her room that night. Certain that the new ghost would visit her, she lay awake for some time, until sleep finally overtook her.

She awoke again with a start to find herself still in darkness in an icy cold room. The chill was familiar, and she fumbled for the matches lying on her bedside table. It was time to light the oil lamp, for her past experiences had taught her that any minute now, her next victim of circumstances was about to make an appearance.

With the lamp flickering at her side, Meredith waited while the room got colder and the silence thickened. Soon she could see it—a pink glow in the corner—growing, darkening, until the center was a fiery red.

Angry swirls coiled around in a flurry of whirlpools until gradually, a figure began to form in the middle of it all. Dark and black it rose, until Meredith could see it was a man.

Her heart began pounding and she clutched the eiderdown to her chin. This was no friendly ghost, as the others had been. This was a man convulsed with rage, with flashes of lightning shooting out in every direction and his fist raised in the air in violent protest.

As always, she could hear no sound from the apparition, but she could feel the energy pulsing into the room, driven by the terrible fury of her unwelcome visitor.

"Who are you?" she whispered. "What do you want of me?"

The head turned in her direction, and now she could see his face. Handsome, even in anger. Young, with piercing blue eyes and an aristocratic nose. For a moment she saw a softening of his features, and then the torment returned, distorting his face once more.

He raised both hands, the fingers outstretched like claws, threatening her so that she drew back. Fright made her voice sharp as she flung a command at him. "Go away! I can't help you. Leave me alone!"

He seemed not to understand, since he drew even closer, his lips drawn back and teeth bared.

Meredith reached for the small clock she kept by the bedside. Raising her hand she hurled it at the ghost, yelling, "Go away! Leave me alone!"

The clock flew through the apparition and hit the dresser behind with a thump before crashing to the floor. At the sound, the figure began to blur, the mist curling around as if to protect him. Then the red faded to pink, and the cloud shrunk to a puff of pink smoke, and disappeared.

Moments later, while Meredith was still trying to quell the tremors that shook her body, a loud rapping on her door made her leap up in fright.

"Meredith? Are you all right?"

It was Felicity's voice, sharp with concern. Meredith scrambled out of bed, snatching up her dressing gown before rushing to the door. She flung it open and dragged a startled Felicity into her room.

"Whatever is it? You're as white as a . . . oh, Lord." Felicity's sharp gaze raked Meredith's face. "You've seen it again."

Meredith nodded, then drew her friend over to the bed

and sank down on the edge. "It was awful. A man, and he was enraged. Quite terrifying, actually."

"Of course," Felicity said, her voice heavy with malice. "What else can you possibly expect from a man— selfish, arrogant beasts."

"I just didn't expect . . ." Meredith shivered, and drew her dressing gown closer around her throat.

"It was bound to happen sooner or later." Felicity sat down next to her. "After all, your first ghost was Kathleen, our dear departed teacher and friend, and the second was an innocent little girl. It was only a matter of time before you conjured up a man."

Meredith bristled. "I did not conjure up anyone. He came to me. If I had any choice in the matter, I would much prefer to be left alone. This ghost business is becoming quite a nuisance."

"That's putting it mildly." Felicity yawned. "I did warn you what would happen if you insisted on helping the other two. If there is such a thing as the spirit world, obviously the word has spread that there is a misguided woman down below who's willing to risk life and limb to help whoever has died in questionable circumstances. No doubt they are all jostling each other to be the next in line."

Meredith gave her a sharp look. "This is no laughing matter, Felicity. This man could be dangerous."

"My dear friend, all men are dangerous. Believe me, I have good reason to know that."

The sour expression on Felicity's face was a familiar one. Meredith had always known that her friend had no time for any man, and had often felt the urge to ask her why.

The thought of lying alone in the dark, afraid to go

to sleep for fear of nightmares, gave her the courage to broach the subject. Perhaps, if she kept Felicity talking for a little while longer, her nerves would settle.

Treading carefully, she murmured, "I wish I knew why you harbor such ill will toward your fellow man."

Felicity slid a sideways glance at her. "Man being the operative word. I have nothing against women or children."

"Then why, Felicity? What happened to you that made you detest every man on earth, good or bad?"

Felicity sniffed. "There is no such thing on earth as a good man."

"Oh, come now. Must you be so judgmental?"

"When it comes to men, yes." Felicity looked down at her hands, clasped together in her lap. "Very well. I suppose I should have told you before now. I must ask, however, that you never pass this on to a living soul."

"Of course. I promise." Meredith settled herself in a more comfortable position. "Now tell me what happened."

For a long moment Felicity sat in silence, until Meredith began to fear she had changed her mind after all.

The room grew quiet and still as they sat in the flickering shadows of the oil lamp, making Meredith nervous once more. She glanced over to the corner of the room, half expecting to see the red mist, but then Felicity stirred and sighed.

"Remember I told you I was the only girl in the family, and that I had four older brothers?"

"Yes." There was something in the teacher's voice that made Meredith begin to wish she hadn't been so hasty in broaching the subject. Feeling guilty, she murmured, "You don't have to tell me if it would upset you to do so."

"No, I want to." Felicity puffed out a breath that seemed to shudder as it passed her lips. "It's just that I have kept the memories shuttered for so long, I had forgotten how painful they could be."

"I'm sorry, I—"

As if afraid she might falter, Felicity cut her off. "My father . . . was a despicable monster. He idolized the boys, but made use of me. He did some awful things to me that . . ."

Her voice trailed off, and Meredith let out a cry of distress. "My dear, I'm so sorry. Let's not talk of it anymore. I understand now. I should never—"

"No, there's more." Felicity laid a hand briefly on her arm. "My brothers knew what was going on and never lifted a hand to help me. In fact, they treated it all as a joke, as if I were a toy to be played with and tossed aside."

Horrified and shaken to the core, Meredith fought back tears. With all her heart she wished she'd listened to her instincts and never asked her friend about her past. Before she could speak, however, Felicity spoke again.

"You know I came to Bellehaven as a pupil years ago."

"Yes, I remember. You mentioned it when I hired you."

"I loved my time here as a student. It was the first time I felt safe, surrounded by females and not a male in sight. Well, except for the maintenance staff and I rarely saw them."

"You were a good student by all accounts."

Felicity's smile was sad. "I devoured everything I was taught, but I loved literature and languages more than anything. The books allowed me to escape into another world, and the ability to speak in another language gave me a sense of power somehow. As if I could say what I wanted without fear of being punished for it."

"And then you had to leave."

"Yes." Felicity's face grew bitter once more. "When I returned to my home, there was someone waiting for me. My father had chosen who he considered to be a suitable husband for me." She shuddered. "He was repulsive, Meredith. Older than my father, fat as a pig and he stank of sweat and cigars."

"Oh, my dear. How utterly awful."

"I simply refused to have anything to do with the man. My father told me if I didn't marry the man he'd chosen for me, then I was to leave his house and never come back. He said I was a disgrace to the family and they wanted nothing more to do with me."

Meredith gasped. "How dreadful. What about your mother? Couldn't she intervene?"

Felicity made a sound of disgust. "She was terrified of my father. She stood by and never uttered a word. I swore from that day on that I would have nothing more to do with a man. Any man. I spent the next five years in service, and every miserable year of it strengthened my vow. I will never give a man power over me again."

"Not all men are that evil."

Felicity sighed. "They are all capable of evil. Look at your ghost. Obviously you sense evil surrounding him."

"I sensed anger. It's not the same thing."

"Well, how fortunate was the day when I came back to visit my tutor and found you instead."

"I often wondered why you had wasted so many years in service when you were so well educated and proficient. I just had a feeling that you had suffered some kind of tragedy, and that you deserved a chance to begin a new life."

"And for that I shall adore you forever." Felicity rose, and now her smile was brighter. "I shall never be able to repay you for giving me this opportunity, Meredith. I can honestly say that I have never been happier."

"That's all the reward I need." Meredith got to her feet. "Besides, you have been a good friend. You've helped me deal with these wayward spirits, even though you don't really believe in them."

"Well, I should warn you, if this man continues to haunt you and you decide to help him, you may well have to do it alone this time."

Meredith suppressed a shiver. "I hope he doesn't return. I really don't want to see him again."

Felicity walked over to where the clock lay in pieces on the floor. Picking them up, she murmured, "Judging by the way you attacked him, I should think he would know better than to try again."

"I hope so." Meredith took the pieces of her broken clock from her and laid them on the dresser.

"Will you be all right?"

Felicity looked worried and Meredith smiled. "Yes, I think so. You can go back to bed." She walked with her friend to the door. "Thank you for telling me about your past. I understand now why you feel the way you do. Nevertheless, I think it's a shame. You have condemned so many good people who are completely without fault."

"Dear Meredith. Always the optimist." Felicity opened the door and added in a whisper, "Be careful, my friend. They are all painted with the same brush." With that, she closed the door, leaving Meredith staring thoughtfully into space.

Chapter 4

"I don't think you're going to get enough girls to stage a protest." Grace shoveled coal through the open oven door, then slammed it shut. "There's only you, me, and three others. What kind of protest is that?"

"We'll get more." Olivia puffed out her breath as she carried a heavy cauldron of hot water to the sink. "We just have to talk to more girls, that's all."

"Some of them are afraid of getting into trouble."

"Yeah, well those are the ones we don't need." Olivia poured the water into the sink, enveloping herself in a cloud of steam. Carrying the empty pot back to the stove she added, "What we need to do is talk to them when they've gone to their rooms at night. When none of the teachers are around to hear us."

Grace wiped her hands on her apron, leaving a smudge of coal dust down the front. "You know we're not allowed near the rooms at night."

"We're not supposed to be protesting either, but that doesn't stop us."

"What if we get caught? That will put an end to the protest, won't it."

"We won't get caught." Olivia wagged a finger at her. "Tonight. That's when we'll do it. We'll go to the rooms tonight and ask the girls to join the protest."

Grace caught her breath. "Tonight?"

"We've only got four days left. It has to be tonight."

"Four days for what?"

Both girls swung around as someone spoke from the doorway.

The chubby woman who entered the kitchen stared at both girls with suspicion etched on her round face. "What are you two up to now?"

"N-nothing, Mrs. Wilkins," Grace stammered, shooting a guilty look at Olivia.

Olivia merely shrugged. "Four days until our day off. We're going down to the village to watch them dance around the maypole."

Mrs. Wilkins frowned. "Did Miss Fingle say you could both have the day off together?"

Olivia sidled up to the cook and nudged her shoulder. "Not exactly. We thought you could put a word in for us. After all, it's May Day. They've got a fete in the vicarage gardens and everything. It wouldn't be fair if one of us could go and not the other, now would it."

The cook glanced at Grace, who immediately dropped her gaze. "Well, I'm not promising nothing, mind you, but I'll talk to Miss Fingle."

Olivia flung her arms around Mrs. Wilkins's shoulders. "I knew you would! I told, Grace, didn't I. I said you were a lovely, kind lady who would want us to have a nice day off to see the dancers."

Mrs. Wilkins shook her off. "Go on with you," she said gruffly, but she smiled when she said it. "Now get on with the washing up. Those dishes have been sitting around for far too long."

"Yes, Mrs. Wilkins." Olivia grinned at Grace and turned back to the sink.

The cook crossed the floor to the pantry and disappeared inside.

Letting out her breath, Grace opened a dresser drawer and pulled out a tea towel. She joined Olivia at the sink and began drying a plate from the pile Olivia had stacked on the draining board. "What if Mona won't let us go?" she whispered.

Olivia frowned at her. "We'll go anyway. It's Saturday, and Mona usually goes to visit her sister in Witcheston. We'll be home again before she gets back. She'll never know we've been gone."

"Mrs. Wilkins will know."

"Know what?"

Grace jumped as the cook spoke from behind her.

"You'll know what's the best time to go to the fete," Olivia said, placing another wet dish on the pile.

"I hope you two are not planning to join up for another of those ridiculous protests," Mrs. Wilkins said, sounding cross. "I should think you've had more than enough trouble with them as it is."

Olivia opened her eyes wide. "What us? No fear. We're not going anywhere near the WSPU, are we, Grace?"

Grace shook her head.

Seemingly satisfied, the cook moved back to the table and began chopping rhubarb sticks into small pieces.

Unnerved by the exchange, Grace picked up another wet plate and almost dropped it as it began to slide through her fingers. So far they had managed to avoid the awkward questions, but she had a nasty feeling that this whole protest thing was going to cause far more trouble than it was worth.

"How utterly dreadful!" Seated in the teacher's lounge in her favorite spot near the fireplace, Essie stared at Meredith, her eyes wide with horror. "What a terrible ghost! I'm so glad you sent him packing."

"I just hope he stays away." Meredith shuddered. "I really don't think I could endure much more of his antagonism. Whoever killed that man surely had good cause."

"Which would put you in an awkward spot," Felicity observed from behind the weekly newspaper. "After all, you helped the other ghosts in order to see justice served, am I right?"

"Quite right. Usually, if a ghost has some unresolved issues, it cannot cross over to the other side. I just tried to resolve the issues for them." Meredith reached for her knitting. The steady clack of needles always seemed to soothe her, and her nerves needed steadying.

She'd had trouble concentrating on her morning classes. Her students, sensing her digression, had become restless and inattentive, making it a difficult morning. She needed to pull herself together before the afternoon sessions.

"Well, then," Felicity said, opening the newspaper to the center pages, "if your ghost had been disposed of with just cause, then you would have a problem. His issues would likely be unsavory ones."

Meredith hooked her strand of wool between her fingers and began knitting a row of purl stitches. "Possibly. In any case, I have no intention whatsoever of helping someone with such an ill temper."

Essie clapped her hands. "I'm very glad to hear it."

Deciding it was time to change the subject, Meredith glanced at the clock on the mantelpiece. "Has anyone seen Sylvia this morning? She is usually in here by now."

"Oh, for goodness sake, don't wish her upon us." Felicity rattled the newspaper. "She is such a ninny. It's impossible to have an intelligent conversation when she's here."

As if to answer her, the door swung open. "I'm so sorry I'm late." Sylvia Montrose entered the room. "I was waylaid by a student with a rather pressing problem."

Essie smiled at the newcomer, while Felicity merely grunted and hid her face behind the newspaper.

"It's quite all right, Sylvia." Meredith moved over on the settee to give the instructress room to sit. "We didn't have any important items to discuss, so you missed nothing."

"Well, we might have one," Felicity said, lowering the newspaper. "Apparently there is a national dart match being held at the Dog and Duck on Saturday."

"Oh, yes." Meredith suffered a guilty start. "I meant to mention it to you all. Mr. Hamilton told me about it yesterday. I'm afraid it slipped my mind."

Felicity gave her a knowing look. "Hamilton was here?"

"Yes." Meredith shifted uneasily on her seat, praying that Felicity wouldn't utter one of her meaningful remarks. Her friend delighted in teasing Meredith about her relationship with the Bellehaven's owner, in spite of her assertions that her association with the man was purely professional.

Fortunately, this time Felicity refrained from commenting on the topic. "Well," she said, holding up the newspaper, "according to this, the village will be inundated with young louts from London, all looking for fun, frolic, and mischief, no doubt."

Sylvia arranged herself on the couch. She wore a green silk waist that complemented the red tints in her blond hair, and her face looked as smooth and flawless as the pages of a brand-new sketch pad. "Oh, dear," she murmured. "That could cause a problem for our girls. Most of them go into the village on Saturdays."

"It's May Day, as well," Essie put in. "I'm sure our students will want to see the maypole dancing and visit the fete."

Felicity frowned at Meredith. "What shall we do about this?"

"I hadn't really thought." Meredith forced her mind off Stuart Hamilton and focused on the problem at hand. "I suppose, under the circumstances, we should establish a curfew."

Felicity frowned. "I think it would be prudent to place the entire village off limits for the day."

Essie uttered a cry of dismay. "The students won't like that, Felicity. They were looking forward to celebrating May Day with the villagers."

"I do think that is a little drastic, Felicity." Meredith turned to Sylvia, more out of courtesy than because she valued her opinion. "What do you think, Sylvia?"

Sylvia pinched her lips. It was obvious from her expression that she agreed with Felicity's suggestion, but was reluctant to acknowledge it. "What did Mr. Hamilton suggest?"

"He left it to me to decide."

Felicity sniffed. "That's a first." She got up and thrust the newspaper at Meredith. "Well, there. Take a look at the account for yourself. It gives a clear picture of what to expect come Saturday."

Reluctantly, Meredith put down her knitting and took the newspaper from her. Opening it, she scanned the lines of the article. Even given the reporter's probable exaggeration for sensation's sake, the account did seem rather alarming.

At least a hundred or so men were expected at the pub, all of them presumably indulging in beer and spirits, free to roam the village once their turn at the dartboard had been accomplished.

A vision of her vulnerable students surrounded by a crowd of leering drunks made her shiver. "Very well, we will put the village off limits for the duration of the dart match."

"Which will be the entire day and evening," Felicity confirmed.

Meredith sighed. "Yes, I suppose. I'll make the announcement at assembly tomorrow morning."

Sylvia nodded, as if it were her idea. "I'm glad to hear it. Is there anything else on the agenda?"

Meredith shook her head. "I suppose we should make our way to the dining room. The bell will ring for the midday meal any moment now."

"Then if you'll excuse me?" Sylvia got up and smoothed the folds of her navy skirt. "I have something I need to do before sitting down to eat."

"By all means."

Felicity watched the young teacher leave, her brow furrowed with irritation. She waited for the door to close, then stuck her finger up under her chin. "I have something I need to do," she said, copying Sylvia's lisp as she attempted to imitate her high-pitched voice. "Bosh, woman. Why can't she just say that she has to pay a visit to the lavatory?"

Essie exploded with laughter. "Felicity! How do you know that?"

"She was fidgeting on the settee with one eye on the clock. Simple deduction, my dear Watson."

Shaking her head, Meredith was about to close the newspaper when a photograph caught her eye. The face seemed familiar, and she took a closer look. Recognizing the features, she uttered a sharp cry and let go of the newspaper. It fluttered to the floor, lying open at her feet. She looked up to see both women staring at her.

"Whatever is it?" Essie cried, leaning forward to get a look at the pages.

Felicity just sat there, her eyebrows raised in question.

"The photograph," Meredith said, pointing down at the newspaper. "That man there. I recognize him. It's my angry ghost!"

Essie gasped and drew back, but Felicity dived forward and snatched up the newspaper.

"His name is Lord James Stalham," she announced, after reading through the lines of newsprint.

Essie gasped again. "You have an aristocrat visiting you, Meredith. How splendid!"

"Not so splendid." Felicity looked up. "The reason his picture is in the paper is because the country estate, owned by his father, is up for sale. Only a skeleton staff remain in the house until it is sold."

"Oh, dear." Essie clasped her hands to her chest. "How sad. His father must have been devastated by his son's death and put the country home up for sale because he couldn't bear to live with the memories."

"Not exactly." Felicity closed the pages of the newspaper. "Stalham's father was found shot to death in the library of the home last winter. Lord Stalham, your angry ghost, Meredith, was hanged a week ago for the murder."

Shock took Meredith's breath away. Before she could recover, the clanging of a bell echoed softly in the corridor outside.

Felicity folded the newspaper and stood. "You must remember Lord Stalham's murder, Meredith. It was in the paper. Remember, we all wondered at the time if his ghost would visit you."

"I remember," Meredith said faintly. She got to her feet, feeling a trifle unsteady. "I don't remember anything about a trial, though."

"That's because it was held in London." Felicity handed her the newspaper. "If there had been any mention of it at all in the *Witcheston Post*, it would most likely have been a small paragraph tucked away somewhere. Until now, of course. There appears to be a full account of the trial in here."

Meredith took the newspaper and tucked it under her arm. She would read it later, she decided, when she had time to absorb it. "Well, we had better get along to the dining room. Sylvia will be wondering what has become of us."

"What will you do if that dreadful ghost comes back?" Essie's eyes glistened with tears. "What a ghastly man— to kill his own father. How utterly beastly."

"I will turn him away," Meredith said, with a confidence she didn't feel. "Eventually he will get tired of bothering me and will go and find someone else to pester."

Essie seemed less than comforted, but she followed Felicity out into the hall without another word. Meredith followed more slowly, greatly disturbed by what she had learned. She prayed that the ghost would not return, for she had not the slightest idea how to behave toward him.

The idea of a murderer in her bedroom, even a dead one, terrified her. She had read somewhere that ghosts cannot physically hurt anyone, yet that did little to reassure her.

She had felt the force of the ghost's fury the night before, and the intensity of it still haunted her.

She wished she knew more about the spirit world, and exactly how much power a ghost could possess. It might have helped prepare her for any more unearthly visits. For she had no doubt at all that this particular ghost fully intended to appear again, and had no intention of leaving her alone until she had done its bidding.

Chapter 5

Grace shivered as she crept along the corridor behind Olivia. Most of the coal fires had been allowed to die down, and a cold draft whisked around her ankles.

They were in the upstairs corridor, forbidden to them after hours. If they were seen, Grace could well imagine Mona Fingle's temper. The housekeeper's real name was Monica, but Olivia had named her Mona because she was always moaning and complaining about the work they did.

Twice already, she'd come close to throwing them out. If it hadn't been for Mrs. Wilkins, both Grace and Olivia would be out of a job by now. Grace pulled her shawl tighter around her shoulders. She didn't know what she'd do if she couldn't work at Bellehaven House. She had no parents. They had both died of consumption.

She had two aunts and a grandmother, all living up north, but she had no desire to go and live with any of them. She knew what it would be—she'd be doing all the housework with no money of her own, having to prove over and over how grateful she was to them for taking her in. No, thank you.

She could always work in London. There were plenty of jobs for housemaids up there. But she'd heard so many stories of horrible things happening to young girls in the city. She could end up in a household where they treated her like dirt. Not like here at Bellehaven, where everyone was kind to her. Everyone except Mona Fingle, that was.

Thinking of Mona made her feel nervous again. She scuttled forward, needing to be closer to Olivia, but just at that moment Olivia stopped, and she bumped into her. There was an awful thud as Olivia's head banged against the door.

"Ouch!" Her yell echoed down the hallway, and Grace winced, waiting for the tirade she knew was coming. Before Olivia could deliver it, however, the door flew open.

Sophie Westchester stood in the doorway and stared in astonishment at the two maids. "What on earth are you two doing here? Don't you know you're not allowed up here after lights out?"

"Shush!" Olivia glared at Grace, then looked down the hallway, where other doors had opened and curious heads were peeking out. "Now look what you've done," she muttered.

"Sorry." Grace gave Sophie a nervous smile. "I sort of bumped into her."

Olivia shook her head, then beckoned to the other girls with a wave of her hand. "Come and listen to this," she called out softly. "I've got something exciting to tell you all."

Some of the students withdrew their heads and closed the doors, but a few of them ventured out into the corridor, huddling together and looking a little fearful.

Quickly Olivia explained about her protest, while Grace stared down the corridor for any sign of an approaching adult.

"What if we get caught?" one of the girls demanded.

"We won't get caught. There's only one bobby and he'll be busy watching over the dancing on the green."

A chorus of voices answered Olivia, while others hissed and shushed to silence them. The whispered arguments went back and forth, and all the time Grace kept her gaze on the end of the corridor.

Finally, some of the pupils agreed to meet Olivia in front of the Dog and Duck on Saturday. "If we get into trouble, mind you," Sophie said, wagging her finger at Olivia, "you'll be the one who takes the blame."

"We won't—" Olivia began, but at that moment Grace thought she saw movement at the top of the stairs.

"Someone's coming," she whispered urgently.

The girls gasped and fled for their rooms, while Sophie grabbed Olivia's arm. "Quick. In here!" She pulled the maid inside the room and beckoned to Grace. "Hurry up!"

Grace tumbled inside the room, followed by three other students, and the door slammed shut behind them.

"Get under a bed," Sophie ordered, "and don't come out until I tell you."

Grace needed no further argument. She wriggled under the bed, and squeezed over as close as she could get to the wall.

Across the room she saw Olivia roll under another bed, and one of the students sat down on the edge of it.

Moments later a loud rapping on the door made Grace jump.

From where she lay she could see just the bottom part

of the door, but she recognized the pointed toes and thick laces of Mona's black shoes.

Heart pounding, she hunched even closer to the wall and drew her knees up to her chin. She heard Sophie explain that one of the girls thought she had seen a mouse in the corridor and they were out there looking for it.

Grace was really impressed, certain she could never think that quickly. Olivia could always think of an answer, but when faced with awkward questions and potential for trouble, Grace invariably became tongue-tied.

It seemed ages while she stared at the pointed shoes, until finally, they backed away and the door closed again. Even so, she waited until she saw Olivia climb out from under her bed before venturing out herself.

After exchanging promises to meet on Saturday, the two maids left the room and hurried down the corridor. It seemed they'd had yet another narrow escape. How many more, Grace thought, as she followed Olivia back down the stairs, before their luck ran out and she'd be out of work? It seemed that day drew closer by the minute.

Meredith opened her eyes and sat up, clutching the bedcovers under her chin. She had been dreaming of floating down the river in a canoe. All had seemed tranquil and pleasant, until the waters had begun to move faster, churning and heaving the boat about, while ahead a cascade of ice and snow awaited her.

Still shivering, Meredith blinked to rid herself of the nightmare. Then, as she was about to settle down again, a corner of the room began to glow.

"No," she whispered. "Go away. I don't want to see you."

The glow thickened to a mist, angry red in the center fading to pink at the edges.

Meredith eyed the door, considering the idea of simply leaving the room, but before she could make a decision, the bad-tempered ghost had appeared before her. He seemed to be mouthing words at her, none of which she could understand. For a moment, that intrigued her.

As a child, in order to learn what grownups were talking about after she'd been banished from their presence, she had learned to read lips.

What she had subsequently learned from the feat was that it doesn't always pay to know what others are saying about you. It was a trick that she had found useful in later life, however, especially in her duties as headmistress.

She had become quite adept at it. In which case, it surprised her that she was unable to read the lips of the ghost, which she could otherwise see quite plainly. Her powers, such as they were, had not improved since her last encounter with an apparition.

The fact that she couldn't understand him seemed to agitate the ghost even more. His face grew distorted, and his eyes appeared to flash fire as he gestured with his hand.

Meredith drew back, wishing she had something else to throw at him. It had seemed to work the night before. The broken clock, however, had been given to Reggie, the maintenance man, to repair, and the only other object on her bedside table was the oil lamp, which she had purposefully left lit before falling asleep earlier. Just in case the ghost should return.

Staring at it now, she mustered up her courage. Using her sternest of voices, she glared at him. "I know who you are, Lord Stalham, and I refuse to help you. No matter what you do or say." Very brave of her, she thought, considering she had no idea what powers he possessed.

For a moment or two flashes of lightning shot out from the mist, blurring the man's image for a moment, then gradually he became clear once more. Holding up his hand, he tilted his head to one side and stuck out his tongue.

Incredibly childish, Meredith thought, but then she realized what he was trying to portray. "Yes," she said, "I know you were hanged for the murder of your father. I read all about it in the newspaper. Well, let me tell you, I believe you got exactly what you deserved. Shooting your own father in cold blood. How despicable."

The ghost shook his head, and waved his hands in front of his face.

Feeling a little braver now that it seemed he could not hurt her after all, Meredith leaned forward. "I do not aid and abet murderers," she said, emphasizing each word. "It seems to me that justice was served, and served well. I do not know why you are unable to leave this world, but you must work that out for yourself. I can't and I won't help you."

Again the ghost shook his head, then raised his fists. The mist grew darker, fiercer in color, while it seemed that flames circled the man's head. Then gradually it faded and once more the fog curled inward, growing smaller until it vanished altogether.

Meredith held her breath until the last wisp of smoke had disappeared, then gave a decisive nod. That should be that. She had twice denied him. Surely now he would leave her alone.

She expressed as much to Felicity and Essie the following morning, while they enjoyed a cup of hot tea in the teacher's lounge.

Essie clapped her hands in approval, though Felicity shook her head and muttered, "If you ask me, you are biting off more than you can chew. If you don't take care, these apparitions that you profess to see will turn your brain. I should hate to see you committed to an asylum."

Meredith felt a cold pang of fear. Although she would never admit it aloud, she had at times doubted her sanity when confronted by the visions. The fact that she had helped to solve two murders had given her some comfort. At least, if she were on the brink of madness, some good had come of it.

"Nonsense." Essie stared at Felicity in dismay. "How could you say such a thing! You know very well that Meredith has more intelligence and common sense than you and I combined."

Felicity laughed. "I don't doubt that, Essie. I just fear that our dear friend can only take so much before she loses the ability to distinguish between reality and fantasy."

"I'm still in the room," Meredith pointed out mildly. "I wish you would not speak of me as if I'm not here." She picked up her knitting bag and opened it. "In any case, I shall make every effort to hold onto my sanity, no matter how many ghosts I encounter."

"Well, let's hope you've seen the last of this one." Felicity leaned back in her chair and crossed her feet. "Though he does seem convinced you can help him. Perhaps he is trying to atone for his sins, in the hope that it will allow him to enter whatever strange world these beings inhabit."

Unsure if Felicity was having fun with her, Meredith clicked her needles in a frenzy of knitting. "I don't see how he can atone for murdering his own father in cold blood."

"Well, no doubt you will soon be telling me he has returned. I have a feeling you won't be rid of him until you've agreed to help him." Felicity laced her fingers together. "Whether this phantom is a figment of your imagination or a visitation from the other side, it seems to me that the matter can only be resolved when you have produced a logical conclusion to an unresolved issue."

Felicity's words remained with Meredith through much of the morning, in spite of her best efforts to ignore them. Perhaps, she thought, as she thankfully headed for the dining room at midday, there just might be some truth in her friend's sentiments. Perhaps she had been too hasty in her refusals to help the ghost of Lord Stalham.

Deep in thought, she was about halfway through her meal of ham, pickles, and cheese when she noticed a great deal of whispering going on in the dining room. Not only at her table, but at the other tables as well.

When she focused on the students, however, they quickly turned the subject to that afternoon's lecture on the celebrated artist, Monet, and Meredith was left with the feeling that whatever had stirred the interest of her pupils, it was something they didn't wish to discuss with her.

Most likely they had been complaining among themselves about the village being off limits for the May Day festivities.

She'd certainly heard many murmurs of shock and dismay when she had made the announcement at assembly that morning.

Normally that would concern her, but today her thoughts were distracted by her preoccupation with the late Lord Stalham's dilemma. So much so that instead of joining her friends in the teacher's lounge, she returned to her office, with the intention of reading the full report on the murder trial.

When she opened the door to her office, however, the sight that met her eyes drove all thoughts of the ghost out of her mind.

Roger was seated behind her desk as usual, and he sprang to his feet as she entered, dislodging the young woman who had been seated on his lap.

Sophie Westchester fell to the floor, her skirts raised in a disgusting display of bare knees. "Ow!" The student glared up at Roger, then scrambled to her feet, her cheeks glowing as she met Meredith's horrified stare. "I . . . we . . . I was just asking Rog . . . Mr. Platt . . ."

"Go to your room." Meredith flung a hand at the door. "And stay there until I come and have a word with you."

"Yes, Mrs. Llewellyn." Bowing her head, Sophie rushed past her and out of the door.

Roger Platt's face had grown as red as a ripe strawberry, and once more he seemed to be having a problem with his starched collar. Tugging at it, he avoided her gaze while he muttered, "I can explain."

"I certainly hope you can." Meredith beckoned to him to move out from her desk and marched behind it herself to sit down.

"Please begin your explanation, and I warn you, your employment here depends on what you have to say."

"Well, I was working here on the housekeeping accounts"—he gestured at the papers strewn across his desk—"when Sophie . . . ah . . . I mean, Miss Westchester, walked in and sat on the edge of my desk." He cleared his throat. "She said she wanted to ask me about the fund for the new art studio. She said some of the girls were discussing a new way to raise money for it."

Meredith frowned. "How did that require her sitting on your lap?"

Roger coughed and tugged at his collar again. "I was showing her the ledger, m'm, and she leaned over to look at it and . . . sort of . . . fell."

"And you expect me to believe that?"

"It's what happened." Roger put a hand over his heart. "I swear it on my dead mother's grave."

Meredith rolled her eyes. "You don't know who your mother is, Roger. You grew up in an orphanage."

"Yes, I know, but I had to have a mother somewhere, right?"

"For all you know, she could be alive and well."

Roger nodded. "I certainly hope so, m'm."

Realizing she had strayed from the issue, Meredith pinched her lips. "You do understand that Miss Westchester deliberately engineered this incident to suit her own purposes?"

"I suppose so, m'm."

"And that it was up to you to prevent this sort of behavior?"

"I did my best, m'm." Roger put on an injured expression. "I shot her off my lap."

"Not until I opened the door."

"Which was exactly the moment it all happened." Roger looked hopeful. "Quite a coincidence, that."

Meredith closed her eyes and passed a hand over her forehead. "You may leave, Mr. Platt. Take this ledger with you and finish working on it in the library. I will let you know when you may have my desk again."

"Yes, m'm, Mrs. Llewellyn." Bowing and touching his forehead with his fingers, Roger snatched up the ledger and fled from the room.

Sighing, Meredith took out the newspaper from the top drawer and opened it. The very next time Stuart Hamilton paid her a visit, she would be sure to get things straightened out with him. She'd had quite enough of Roger, Sophie Westchester, and their shenanigans. Roger Platt had to go, and she would demand that Hamilton either find her a new assistant, or she would find one herself.

Chapter 6

"I read the article in the newspaper," Meredith announced, later that afternoon. "It was most interesting."

Essie turned to her, her long skirts blowing around her ankles in the breeze. The warm sunshine had beckoned to her, and she had suggested a short walk in the grounds before returning to their final classes of the day. "Really? What did it say?"

Felicity, who had strode ahead of them as usual, slowed her pace to listen.

Meredith paused in front of a bench at the edge of the flower beds. "Why don't we sit here for a moment. I will tell you what I read."

Essie seated herself, while Felicity looked a little impatient. "I read some of it myself," she said, dropping onto the bench, "until I got to the part where it said James Stalham protested his innocence throughout the trial. Then I gave up in disgust. After all, isn't that what all criminals do? Insist they are innocent of the crime?"

Meredith leaned her back against the bench. It felt good to relax after the difficult confrontation she'd had with Sophie Westchester, who had been quite defiant until Meredith had threatened to have her removed from the school. At which point the student had mumbled a resentful apology and promised to stay away from Roger Platt—a promise Meredith had no doubt the student intended to break at the very next opportunity.

Dismissing the wayward girl from her mind, Meredith raised her chin. It was such a pretty day. Sunlight once more bathed the gray walls of the school, and glistened on the smooth lawns. Beyond where she sat she could see the dark green branches of the poplars swaying, as if they were dancing in the wind.

Above her head birds twittered and fluttered about among the leaves, and the fragrance of freshly cut grass reminded her that summer was not too far away. She was reluctant to spoil such a peaceful scene with talk of a murder, yet she was anxious to share what she had learned in the newspaper article.

"James Stalham did, indeed, protest his innocence." She leaned down to pluck a blade of grass from the hem of her skirt.

"What is more," she added, straightening her back again, "the defense attorney insists that James was innocent and that the judge misled the jury, by not allowing evidence."

"He's paid to say that." Felicity sneezed, and hunted in her sleeve for a handkerchief. "That's what defense attorneys do."

Essie leaned forward, her forehead creased in a frown. "Did the article say what actually happened that night?"

"Yes. James Stalham told the court he was having a

late nightcap in the parlor when he heard a shot. It came from the library, across the hall from him. He rushed in and found his father lying on the floor, with a gun lying next to him. He picked up the gun, put it on the table, and then rang for the constables."

Essie gasped, a hand over her mouth. "How awful."

"Did he say his father shot himself?" Felicity looked skeptical, as Meredith had expected.

"No," she said. "James insisted that someone else shot Howard Stalham. The fact that the only fingerprints found on the gun belonged to James, helped convict him of the crime. The prosecutor maintained that if Howard Stalham had shot himself, his fingerprints would also have been on the gun. If someone else had shot him, the killer would have had to clean the gun, and would still have been in the room when James arrived."

Essie looked confused. "I don't understand all this talk of fingerprints. What does that mean?"

Felicity jumped in to answer. "Oh, come, Essie. Surely you've heard of it? It's the latest technique the constabulary is using to catch criminals. Or rather, it's actually Scotland Yard that is employing the method. They can actually tell the identity of someone by the prints on their fingers."

Essie stared at the tips of her fingers. "You mean these little lines and swirls on them?"

"Well, of course that's what I mean." Felicity held out her own hands. "Every single person in the world has different patterns of those lines and swirls. See? Mine are different from yours."

Essie shook her head. "I still don't see how that can catch a criminal."

"It's obvious, Essie. Take this case of the Stalham

murder. After James Stalham was arrested, the constables inked his fingers and then pressed them to a sheet of paper. That left prints that they matched to the pattern left on the gun."

Essie gazed at Felicity in awe. "How on earth do you know all that?"

"Don't let her overwhelm you with her superior knowledge," Meredith said, with a quick frown at Felicity. "She read it in the newspaper. Just as I did. There was an article about it not too long ago. Apparently Scotland Yard has been officially using the method for at least two years."

"So then," Essie said, frowning in concentration, "if no one else was in the room with Lord Stalham, and only his finger patterns were on the gun—"

"Prints," Felicity interrupted. "Finger*prints.*"

"—how could someone else have shot him?" Essie finished, completely ignoring Felicity for once.

"Precisely." Felicity sighed. "The evidence against James Stalham was overwhelming. According to the butler, no one else was in the house that evening, except the maids and the housekeeper. There were no signs that someone had forced their way into the house, and at the time of the shooting, the staff were all asleep in their rooms."

"Except the butler," Felicity murmured. "Wasn't he the one who found James standing over the body?"

"Yes, he was. He testified at the trial that he'd heard James arguing with his father earlier that evening. Apparently James had gambled away a great deal of money and his father had threatened to disown him."

"Well, that certainly gives James a motive to get rid of the old boy," Felicity said cheerfully. "I can certainly understand how he felt."

Aware that Felicity was referring to her own past experience, Meredith exchanged a significant glance with her before answering. "James declared that his argument with Howard Stalham was over someone called Pauline Suchier, who was apparently Howard's mistress. The butler, however, insisted that James was lying, both about the mistress and the cause of the argument."

"One of them was certainly lying." Felicity shaded her eyes to look at the sun. "I do believe it's time we went back to the school."

Meredith got to her feet, pondering on Felicity's words. *One of them was lying.* But which one? What if Howard Stalham had, in fact, been involved with another woman? What if James had been telling the truth about the argument, that it wasn't about his gambling after all. If so, why would the butler lie about it?

She couldn't be sure why, but something didn't seem quite right. Maybe it was the violent way the ghost of James Stalham had shaken his head when she'd called him a murderer. He was already dead. What did he have to gain now by protesting his innocence? Unless he really had been innocent of the crime and needed to prove it in order to cross over.

Either way, perhaps Felicity was right, after all. Past experience had taught her that a ghost could be quite persistent. James Stalham could prove to be no exception. Besides, now that her curiosity had been aroused, she had to admit she would like to find out more about the case. It intrigued her, and if by chance a miscarriage of justice had occurred, then she just might be able to help James Stalham rest in peace.

* * *

The dinner bell had already rung when Meredith received the word that Stuart Hamilton awaited her presence in the library. Miffed that she would be late for the meal, and therefore would have to endure a cold supper—something she detested—she was not in a good frame of mind when she entered the library.

Hamilton stood by the fireplace, his hands behind his back, his gaze on the flickering flames leaping up the chimney. He turned as she closed the door, and regarded her with a grave expression.

"It has come to my notice," he said, without even bothering to greet her, "that Pratt is in trouble again."

Meredith raised her eyebrows. "Good evening, Mr. Hamilton. May I ask, how did you find out about the incident with Mr. *Platt?*"

If Hamilton had noticed her emphasis on her assistant's correct name, he gave no sign. "Miss Montrose informed me of it."

Meredith tightened her lips. Of course. She might have known. Sylvia Montrose wasted no time in running to Hamilton any time she could find an excuse. "I wonder how Miss Montrose knew enough about the situation to feel confident in passing it along to you."

"Apparently she heard it from one of the students." He tilted his head to one side. "I've had a word with Pratt, and he has given me his sworn oath that he will have nothing more to do with the student in question."

Meredith moved over to the nearest chair and sat down. "I'm afraid that neither Mr. Platt nor Miss Westchester seems able to honor their promises."

"So I've noticed."

Hamilton walked over to the window, and Meredith watched him with a frown. He seemed ill at ease, most unusual for him, since his confidence and assurance usually bordered on arrogance.

"Is something wrong?" she asked tentatively. "Apart from the fact that I have an impetuous assistant who seems bent on causing a great deal of trouble, I mean."

Hamilton turned to face her. "I'm sorry that he is proving to be such a nuisance."

Meredith folded her hands in her lap. "Roger Platt is far more than a nuisance. He refuses to obey my demands that he stay away from the young ladies of this establishment. He apparently fails to realize the effect this kind of behavior could have on their reputations, and possibly even their future lives. The students of Bellehaven are my responsibility, and I simply will not put up with this situation any longer. I must insist that you replace him at once."

Hamilton patted the top pocket of his waistcoat and drew out a cigar. He sniffed it, rolled it in his fingers, then, apparently changing his mind, replaced it in his pocket. "I understand your concerns, Meredith, but I ask you to reconsider. I've acted quite sternly with the young man, and I believe he now understands the gravity of his situation. I beseech you to give him one last chance."

Meredith let out her breath on a puff of resentment. "I have given that incorrigible young man far too many chances. I fail to see how one more can produce a miracle."

Hamilton moved toward her, with a purposeful expression that thoroughly unnerved her. "Meredith, I have something to tell you. Something I should have mentioned before, but I was hoping to confirm everything before I revealed what I know."

Wary now, she watched his face. As always, his gaze

on her put her at a disadvantage. Her heart sped up until she felt as though he would surely see it beating against her chest. She dropped her chin, waiting with shortened breath to hear what he had to say.

He was almost upon her before he halted. She kept her gaze firmly on his highly polished boots, her shoulders braced against the rapid pulsing of blood through her veins.

"I have reason to believe," Hamilton said, in a voice so deep and gruff with emotion it startled her, "that Roger Platt could be my nephew. His mother, my sister, died at his birth. I was studying abroad at the time, and didn't learn of the child's existence until a few years ago."

So intrigued was she that Hamilton had properly used her assistant's name, she almost lost the thread of what he had said next. As it sunk in, however, she looked up, receiving the full force of his gaze.

Her lips felt dry when she spoke. "Oh, I'm so sorry. About the loss of your sister, I mean."

Hamilton gave her a brief nod. "Thank you. I've spent the last six years trying to find the child, who would now be Pratt's age. My research suggests that Pratt *is* that child, but I have yet to receive conclusive evidence. When and if I do, I intend to take him into my home. Since I have no other family members left, he would be my sole relative. Once I have control of him, I have no doubt that I can mold him into a responsible, trustworthy adult."

Staring into the owner's eyes, Meredith had absolutely no doubt he could achieve such an undertaking. For some strange reason, the thought of it pleased her beyond measure. "Oh, my," she breathed. "How fortunate for that young man."

Hamilton leaned in closer. "I certainly hope so. I would

vastly prefer, of course, to have my own natural son and heir. Unfortunately, I have no wife to provide me with a child."

"Of course." Meredith resisted the impulse to fan her face. She was feeling quite faint. It had to be hunger. After all, she was sadly overdue for her evening meal.

"And rest assured, I shall not give up hope on that score. While there's life, there's hope, so they say."

"Oh, indeed." She could barely get the words out. What on earth was the matter with her?

"Meanwhile"—Hamilton straightened, breaking the spell that had held her mesmerized—"I see no harm in welcoming a substitute, just in case that happy event should not occur."

"Quite." The word had come out as a croak, and Meredith cleared her throat. "I understand now why you are so anxious to keep him employed here."

"Precisely. I cannot mention any of this to Pratt, obviously, until I have confirmation that he is indeed my nephew. On the other hand, if he leaves this employ, I might well lose sight of him and will have to hunt him down again. That's why I must ask you to put up with him a little longer, just until I have the proof that I need, one way or another."

Right then she would have agreed to anything he asked. "Very well. I shall have to keep a stern eye on him, of course, but perhaps, if I enroll the other tutors to help, we can keep him out of trouble for a while longer."

"Thank you, Meredith. I shall be eternally grateful." Hamilton held out his hand.

Thinking he meant to help her to her feet, she placed her fingers in his warm palm. Instead, he lifted her hand to his mouth and gently pressed his lips against her skin.

Instantly, she wished she had worn her gloves. In normal circumstances, when visiting with a gentleman, a lady always wore gloves. Since she had been more or less waylaid on her way to the dining room, there had been no time or thought of such proprieties. The touch of his lips on her bare hand, however, was uncommonly intimate.

Pulling her fingers from his grasp, she shot to her feet.

"Well, I'm glad we have that settled. Now, if you will excuse me, I have duties to attend to in the dining room."

"Of course." He stepped back and bowed his head. Just before he did, however, she caught his expression. The smile on his lips was positively wicked.

It took all her attention to regain her composure as she hurried along the corridor to the dining room. Infuriating man.

Just when she thought she had built up a resistance to his dangerous charm, he inevitably found a way to break through her resolve and reduce her to the ridiculous antics of a giddy adolescent.

She had been in the company of too many young women for far too long, she chided herself. This simply would not do. She must strive to have more control over her emotions, and stop behaving like one of her misguided students.

Upset with herself, she ate very little of her meal, and retired to her room early without bothering to give Essie or Felicity an explanation. A good night's rest would refresh her, she assured herself, and had barely settled into her bed before drifting off to sleep.

Much to her surprise and relief, she awoke the next morning, having been undisturbed by a visit from the ghost of Lord Stalham.

Having decided on a course of action, she was anxious to tell Felicity and Essie about her intentions. She had no doubt they would try to dissuade her from her plans, but she was resolved now to follow through with her intent to find out more about the murder, and she needed the cooperation of her friends if she was to have any success at all.

She would simply have to persuade them to accept her decision and trust they would understand why she felt compelled to come to the aid of a convicted murderer.

All she could hope was that Hamilton didn't hear of her investigation. She had enough problems with him as it was, and certainly didn't need any further complications in her association with him. Dealing with her unfortunate and ridiculous infatuation for him was more than enough to keep her on her toes.

Chapter 7

As soon as Meredith entered the teacher's lounge, Essie practically leapt at her. "Well? Did you see him again?"

A quick glance around satisfied Meredith that Sylvia was not in the room. Felicity sat by the window, and although she affected a look of indifference, Meredith could tell that she had her ears pinned back in anticipation of an answer.

"Yes," Meredith said, in as nonchalant a voice as she could manage, "I did. He sent for me right before dinner."

The look on Essie's face was almost comical. Her eyebrows arched in surprise, and her eyes opened so wide the irises looked startlingly blue. "How did he do that?"

Meredith frowned. "He sent a student to tell me he was in the library."

Essie sat down heavily on the chair behind her. "Other people can see him and hear him? Oh, my!"

"Of course they can." Only too well, Meredith added inwardly. "Whatever is the matter with you, Essie?"

Across the room, Felicity chuckled. "She's talking about the ghost, Meredith."

"Oh!" Feeling foolish, Meredith took her seat by the fire.

Apparently her meeting with Hamilton still weighed heavily on her mind. If she wasn't careful, Felicity's shrewd gaze would eventually detect that Bellehaven's owner had more than a casual effect on Meredith's composure, and she'd never hear the last of it.

Rumors could easily arise and reach the ears of Hamilton himself, and that would be utter disaster. She would never be able to face him again.

Doing her best to ignore Felicity's knowing look, Meredith smiled at Essie. "I'm happy to say, Lord Stalham did not put in an appearance last night."

Essie appeared disappointed at the news. "Really? Do you think he has given up on eliciting your help?"

"I certainly hope so. He's not a pleasant fellow at all. Then again, if he has been hanged for a crime he did not commit, I can hardly blame him for being a tad testy."

Felicity groaned. "Don't tell me, Meredith, that you believe James Stalham did not kill his father after all."

"I'm not sure what I believe." Meredith paused, then added in a rush, "I would, however, like to get to the real truth of that matter."

"The real truth is that James has been convicted and hanged for the murder. There's little you can do about it now."

Hearing a warning in Felicity's voice, Meredith frowned. "I can certainly look into it. If someone else killed Howard Stalham, he should pay for the crime, for he would be guilty of taking the lives of not one person, but two."

Essie looked confused. "How so?"

Meredith sighed. "The murder of Howard Stalham and the subsequent execution of his son, James."

"Oh." Essie's brow remained creased. "So what are you going to do about it?"

Meredith glanced at Felicity, wincing at the look of disapproval on her friend's face. "I'm going to pay a visit to the Stalham country estate. This afternoon. I shall give my students an assignment while I'm away."

Felicity pursed her lips. "Are you sure that's wise? Or even necessary? What if your ghost has given up the idea of asking for your help? Your investigation would be a complete waste of time."

"It's never a waste of time to see justice served on the guilty." Meredith rose to her feet. "If a misjudgment has been made, then it should be put right, whether or not James Stalham returns."

"Meredith is quite right," Essie said, nodding her head. "After all, we could have a killer roaming around the village. Just think of the danger our students might face."

"If there is another killer," Felicity said, pushing herself up from her chair, "which I seriously doubt, he would most likely have departed these parts some time ago. Especially if he was well acquainted with the Stalhams, which I suppose he would have to be if he was not obliged to force his way into the house. The Stalhams' main residence is in London, is it not?"

Meredith nodded. "According to the article, they only used the country estate for weekends. Apparently Lord Howard enjoyed hunting, and in fact, he had planned to join a hunting party the next day, had he not died. His wife, Lady Clara, had remained in the city, and was informed of his death the following day."

Essie uttered a cry of distress. "How awful! The poor woman. To lose her husband and her son in such swift succession."

"Indeed. It must be very difficult for her." Meredith walked to the door. "Which is one of the reasons I feel compelled to ferret out what really happened. I intend to pose as a prospective purchaser and ask to look over the estate."

"Don't they have agents for that?"

Meredith smiled at Felicity's frown of concern. "They do, but there is no reason why I shouldn't act on my own. In any case, only a few members of the staff remain in the mansion. I'm sure someone will accommodate me."

"I just hope you know what you are doing."

Without bothering to answer her, Meredith opened the door.

The truth was, she had never been confident in her ability to investigate a crime. It was largely by luck that she had solved the previous two cases, with perhaps just a little perceptive thinking thrown in. She could only hope that her luck held in this event. Just in case the ghost of James Stalham decided to return.

Having ordered Reggie Tupper, her loyal, if somewhat capricious handyman, to bring around the carriage, Meredith waited on the steps for him to arrive. She had dressed conservatively in a black skirt, white lace waist, and black velvet jacket to guard against a cool wind that still bore traces of a departed winter at times.

Her gloves were showing signs of wear, she noticed, as she fastened her silk scarf more securely about her throat. Soon she would have to purchase more. The wide brim of her hat shaded her face, and she tilted her chin at the sound of horse's hooves.

Reggie's face glowed with excitement as he climbed down to open the door for her. Leaning toward her, he whispered hoarsely, "Are we going after another murderer?"

She tried to look surprised. "Goodness, Reggie, whatever makes you think that?"

"You don't usually go out without Miss Cross and Miss Pickard, do you. I thought you might be off on one of your investigations."

"I'm merely going to look at some property that's for sale."

She climbed up onto her seat. "So you can stop speculating about my intentions."

Reggie looked disappointed. "Very well, m'm."

To her relief he closed the door and climbed up onto his seat. She'd had to take the maintenance man into her confidence more than once, but only as a last resort, when she was unable to explain her activities. She saw no reason to enlighten him this time, unless it became absolutely necessary.

The new horse always seemed anxious to be on the move, and at the slightest flick of the reins, lunged into action. The first time or two she had traveled with him, she had been taken unawares and had been thrown back against the back of the seat, dislodging her hat so that it fell over her eyes.

Most annoying, since she had to reset the pesky thing on her head without the benefit of a mirror. She'd spent one entire afternoon shopping in Witcheston with a ribbon dangling down her back and a hat pin swinging on the end of it. No wonder she'd received so many odd glances.

Reggie had named the new horse Spirit, a name she had to admit suited his rambunctious nature, but personally she would rather have had a horse with a little less spirit. She missed the steady plodding of Major, who had been retired once Spirit had taken over the reins.

Watching the fields rush by, Meredith sighed. It seemed that everything nowadays depended on more and more speed. The motorcars that clogged the streets of Witcheston moved so fast these days that she barely had time to cross the road before one was upon her, honking that dreadful horn and spitting out nasty, smelly smoke.

In no time at all, it seemed, Reggie was heading up the driveway to the grand entrance of the Stalham estate. Meredith gathered up her handbag and prepared herself for the jolt when the carriage halted. Even so, she slid forward and had to right herself before Reggie opened the door.

"Here we are, m'm," Reggie sang out, and held out his hand to help her down.

There was a time when she would have thanked him and dismounted without his aid, but the rapid pace of their journey had made her somewhat unsteady, and she accepted the firm support of his arm.

"Goodness," she said, when her feet were solidly planted on the ground, "we certainly kept up a good pace today."

"Yes, m'm." Reggie grinned. "That Spirit really knows how to charge ahead."

"Yes, well, I just hope he doesn't charge us right into a hedge. We were going around the bends a little too fast for comfort."

Reggie's grin widened. "Don't you worry yourself, m'm. I'll make sure we stay on the road."

"I certainly hope so." Meredith glanced up at the main doors. "Wait for me here, Reggie. I shan't be long."

As she mounted the steps, a tumult of raucous barking broke out, from what were obviously very large dogs. They kept up the din while she tugged on the bell rope, and didn't cease their protests until the door opened. A tall, gaunt man stood in the doorway, dressed in a black morning coat and gray striped trousers. His gray hair was swept back from a high forehead, and his nose jutted out at a fierce angle. Dark blue eyes regarded her with just a hint of hostility, beneath sparse eyebrows raised in question.

This, apparently, was Smithers, the Stalhams' butler. "Good afternoon," Meredith said, doing her best not to feel intimidated. After all, the man was nothing more than a servant, though she doubted very much that he'd see it that way.

Since he seemed disinclined to answer, she said briskly, "My name is Mrs. Llewellyn, and I understand this estate is up for sale. I would be very interested in viewing the property, if I may?"

Smithers's nose tilted upward. "You have an appointment?"

Meredith curbed her resentment. The man knew very well she didn't have an appointment. He was, however, entitled to ask for one. "I am visiting the area," she said, placing a pleasant smile on her face. "I happened to hear of the sale, and since I won't be here long, I thought I'd take a chance on this being a convenient time to view the property."

The butler was obviously concerned about losing a possible sale. Of course, he could prefer that the mansion not be sold, thus ensuring he stayed in residence there. On the other hand, no doubt the heirs would keep him employed elsewhere, which could be what he favored.

With all the alternatives running through her mind, Meredith anxiously watched the butler's face. After a long pause, he stepped back and held the door open wider. "I will have Mrs. Parker, the housekeeper, show you over the premises," he announced, after ushering her into the library.

His obvious disapproval of her presence made her uneasy, and she was relieved when he left her alone. Until she remembered that this was the very room in which Howard Stalham had died.

It was a large room, with tall French windows that overlooked a lawn bordered by trees. Seated on a blue satin settee, Meredith stared at the carpet. Lord Stalham had lain there, bleeding profusely no doubt, with his son standing over him.

Had James shot his father in order to avoid being cut off from the family fortune, or had he been telling the truth? Had someone else pulled the trigger and left a dying Howard for his son to find? Meredith suppressed a shiver, and glanced over at a dark corner of the room, half expecting to see a red mist forming with an enraged ghost in the center.

Reassured to see no such thing, she surveyed the room, her gaze coming to rest on the gun cabinet on the opposite wall. Again a shudder rippled down her spine.

Steeling herself, she got up and walked over to the cabinet. The killer must have taken the gun from the cabinet. How easy would it have been for James, in the heat of an argument, to seize the gun from the case and fire at his father? Curious, she took hold of the knob and twisted it.

The door swung open. Surprised, she frowned at the contents. Had it been kept unlocked? If so, it would have been all too easy for James to snatch up the gun. Perhaps she had been hasty in doubting his guilt.

The light tap on the door made her jump. When it opened, a young woman entered carrying a large tray. She appeared to be far too youthful to be entrusted with the tasks of a housekeeper. Though not too young to be with child, affirmed by the swelling in her belly.

"Good afternoon, m'm," she said, coming to a halt a few feet away. "Mrs. Parker sent me to tell you she's been delayed but will be with you shortly. Meanwhile she hopes you will enjoy a cup of tea."

"Thank you." Concerned that the heavy tray might be too much for the maid in her delicate condition, Meredith was tempted to take the load from her. She remembered, just in time, that she was supposed to be a wealthy client looking to buy the mansion, and would never dream of coming to the aid of a lowly servant.

She waited for the maid to put down the tray, then murmured, "So kind of Mrs. Parker." She moved to sit down, while the maid poured a small amount of cream into the fragile china cup.

"One lump or two, m'm?"

"One will be sufficient, thank you."

"Yes, m'm."

Meredith waited another moment or two while the maid extracted a sugar lump from the bowl with a pair of silver tongs, and dropped it into her cup. "Forgive my morbid curiosity," she said, as the young woman poured out a stream of steaming tea, "but I understand your master was killed in this room not too long ago."

The maid jumped, spilling the dark brown liquid into the saucer. With an exclamation of dismay, she put down the teapot, fished a handkerchief out of her apron pocket, and carefully mopped up the puddle before replacing the brimming cup on the saucer.

"Pardon me," Meredith said quickly. "I didn't mean to startle you."

"Oh, that's all right, m'm." The young woman gave her a nervous glance. "I've been really jumpy lately. Dropping all sorts of things. Mrs. Parker says it's because of the baby." She laid a protective hand on her belly. "It messes up me nerves."

"So I remember." Meredith smiled. "What's your name?"

"It's Winnie, m'm."

"Well, Winnie, I was wondering if you could tell me what happened here that night. I noticed the gun cabinet is open. Is it always left unlocked?"

Winnie shot a glance at the gun case. "Yes, m'm. It is. Lord Stalham had a stiffness in his fingers and had trouble turning the key. He got cross one day and threw the key into the fire. The cabinet hasn't been locked since. Though no one's allowed to touch the guns. Except Smithers, of course, and he only touches them once a month when he cleans them."

"Ah, I see. I noticed that some of them are quite old."

The maid offered Meredith a plate of tiny jam tarts filled with lemon curd. "Yes, m'm. One of them belonged to an American bank robber, so I'm told."

"Indeed? How interesting." Meredith took one of the tarts and bit into it. The tangy flavor pleased her, and she quickly finished the tasty morsel.

"Yes, m'm." Winnie shot another uneasy glance at the cabinet. "Lord Stalham kept the gun loaded, too. He frightened me one day when he showed it to an acquaintance of his while I was in the room. Sir Gerald Mackleby, it was. He took the gun from Lord Stalham and was waving it about while he talked. I kept expecting it to go off and shoot me."

"That must have been very disturbing." Meredith sipped her tea and put the cup back on the saucer.

"Yes, m'm. It were. It gave me quite a scare, I can tell you. I remember looking at that gun and thinking something bad was going to happen one day. Blow me if the very next day, Lord Stalham wasn't lying dead on this very floor. Shot by that very gun."

"How awful. Sir Gerald must have been quite shaken by the ordeal."

Winnie shrugged. "I don't know about that, m'm. He weren't here when it happened. He'd gone back to London the night before Lord Stalham got shot."

"It must have been a dreadful shock for everyone here."

Winnie put a hand over her heart. "Oh, it were, m'm. I was in bed, fast asleep when it happened, and I woke up to hear a commotion downstairs. I came down to see what was the matter, just in time to see the bobbies leading Mr. James away. It was really awful."

Meredith nodded in sympathy. "How dreadful for everyone to discover that Lord Stalham had murdered his own father."

There was a long pause before Winnie answered in a whisper. "Dreadful." Her eyes filled with tears. "I never thought Mr. James would be hanged."

"Why?" Meredith leaned forward. "Is it, perhaps, because you don't believe James killed his father?"

Winnie seemed to have trouble replying and Meredith held her breath. Was it possible that the maid knew something that would help uncover the truth about that night?

Watching her intently, Meredith waited for an answer.

Chapter 8

After what seemed an eternity, Winnie gulped. "I don't know what happened. Nobody knows what really happened in here that night. I just know it was the worst night of my life."

Disappointed, Meredith said soothingly, "Well, it's all over now, and you mustn't dwell on it. You have a little one to consider. You and your husband must be so excited about the baby."

Winnie's cheeks grew red and she backed away. "If that will be all, m'm, I must get downstairs to the kitchen. Mrs. Parker will be up here right away."

Meredith was left no time to ponder on Winnie's re-action, since just as the maid reached the door, a thin woman with spectacles and frizzy gray hair appeared in the doorway.

Winnie scuttled past her and out into the hallway.

The housekeeper advanced into the room, and nod-ded at Meredith. "Mrs. Llewellyn, I'm Mrs. Parker, the housekeeper. If you're ready, I'll be happy to show you around."

"Thank you. Very kind of you." Meredith rose, brushing crumbs from her skirt, then followed the housekeeper out into the hallway.

At the end of it, Smithers stood talking to Winnie, who appeared to be cowering in front of him. Mrs. Parker clicked her tongue in annoyance. "If you will pardon me just for one moment, m'm. There is something I must attend to and then I'll be right back."

Meredith nodded, and watched the housekeeper trot down the hallway. Smithers looked up as she approached, and even from that distance Meredith could tell the butler was annoyed about something.

For a moment or two the housekeeper and butler argued back and forth, while Winnie stood staring at the floor. Finally, Smithers flung out a hand and Winnie scampered off. With a parting shot at the housekeeper, Smithers followed her and Mrs. Parker hurried back to Meredith.

"I'm so sorry about that," she said, puffing a little. "Just a little domestic disagreement. It's all taken care of now." She waved a hand at the staircase that curved upward to the next floor. "Would you care to view the bedrooms first?"

"That would be lovely." Following the wiry woman up the stairs, Meredith added, "It must be hard for Winnie to keep up with her chores, considering her condition."

"She does all right. When she doesn't have her nose behind a newspaper, that is. Always reading, that girl." Mrs. Parker paused at the top of the stairs. "It'll get worse for her as time goes on. She doesn't have much choice, though, does she, what with having no husband to take care of her."

Having suspected as much, Meredith merely nodded. "How sad."

"It is sad, and none of it her fault." The housekeeper's features hardened. "She told me the baby's father forced his attentions on her. Such a disgrace. Her life is ruined, and with the father gone she has no chance of anyone taking care of that baby except herself. It's a hard life she has set up for her, I can tell you."

"I'm so sorry." Meredith's heart went out to the poor child. "Can nothing be done to help her?"

Mrs. Parker sniffed. "Not in this house. If you ask me, far too much has been done to her already." She reached a door and opened it. "This is the master suite. I think you'll find it quite cozy, despite its size."

Meredith gave the elegant room only a cursory glance. She was far too intrigued by the housekeeper's comment. "Are you perhaps suggesting that someone in this house is the father of Winnie's baby?"

Mrs. Parker sent her a furtive glance. "Maybe I am and maybe I'm not. There are some who say James was the father, but Winnie won't say as much. She's not one to condemn a dead person."

"But the child could be the legal heir to a fortune."

"It's not what Winnie wants." Mrs. Parker glanced at the door as if afraid someone might be listening behind it. "If you ask me, I think she's afraid that if she does claim James as the father, her baby will be taken away from her and raised by the family and she won't have no say in the matter. Our Winnie is a lot stronger than she looks. She's determined to bring up that child alone."

"I admire her for that." Meredith shook her head. "It won't be easy."

"I'm sure she knows that." Mrs. Parker walked to the

window and drew back the green and gold damask curtains. "There's a lovely view of the gardens from here, if you'd care to take a look."

Meredith joined her at the window. The view was indeed pleasing. A large fountain sat in the center of smooth lawns, which were bordered on either side by high hedges rimmed with flower beds. Wide-spreading oaks gave shelter at the far end and behind them the sun glinted on a large lake, just visible through the trees.

"It's lovely," she murmured. "You must be sad at the thought of all this changing hands."

"Oh, I don't mind at all." The housekeeper drew the curtains back across the window and headed for the door. "I grew up in London, and never was happy when the master moved me down here. Once the estate is sold I'll be moving back into the main house. Lady Clara's housekeeper is retiring, so I'll be taking her place."

"Lady Clara. That's Lord Stalham's wife?"

The housekeeper nodded. "James's mother. Lovely lady, she is. We all love her. Especially Smithers. He worships the ground she walks upon, honest he does. Do anything for her, he would, and that's saying a lot for a man like Smithers. He wouldn't do nothing for nobody else, but Lady Clara . . . well, all she has to do is lift her little finger and Smithers is like a little puppy dog running for a bone."

"He must have been a great comfort to her then, after the murder."

"Oh, indeed he was. Poor woman. She was heartbroken over the loss of her son."

Following the housekeeper out into the hall, Meredith murmured, "And no doubt the loss of her husband, as well."

Mrs. Parker pinched her lips. "Oh, I don't think there was much love lost there. Howard Stalham was a hard, cruel man. Though I shouldn't speak ill of the dead." She made a quick sign of the cross on her chest.

"He wasn't well liked, then?"

The housekeeper paused in front of another door and threw it open. "We were all afraid of him. He could be really cruel. He once whipped a young stable boy for no good reason at all. The master had ordered his horse to be saddled, and wouldn't listen when the boy told him the horse was ailing. The boy saddled a different horse anyway, and the master was furious. He took a whip to him, and made him saddle the horse that was ill. The poor thing died a week later. That boy still has the scars of that whipping, and never got over it."

"Does the boy still work here?"

The housekeeper pushed open the door. "No, he left a while ago. This is another of the bedrooms. Not as big as the master suite, but very cozy all the same."

Meredith glanced around. "Very nice. Tell me more about the stable boy. Was he still working here when Lord Stalham was shot?"

The housekeeper gave her a sharp glance. "No, he wasn't. He ran off one night and never came back. That was months before the shooting." She frowned. "I know there's some who don't believe James shot his father, but I can assure you, that stable boy was far from here when it happened."

Meredith met her gaze squarely. "Do *you* believe James killed his father?"

Mrs. Parker turned sharply and marched out into the hallway.

She waited for Meredith to follow her out then closed the door with a soft thud. "All I'll say is that someone else was in the house that night. I don't know who but I know someone was here all right."

"But Smithers testified that only the staff was here that night, besides James and his father, that is."

The housekeeper set off at a fast pace toward the end of the hallway. "Maybe he didn't know. He refuses to talk about it so who knows what he knew."

Meredith hurried to catch up with her. "But if there was someone else in the house that night, why didn't someone say something? Why didn't *you* testify?"

"Because the lawyer wouldn't let me. He said since I couldn't say who it was for certain, I couldn't say it in court. He said that Smithers was the only one who knew what really happened. All the rest of us were in our rooms fast asleep. I didn't know anything was wrong until the dogs' barking woke me up. When I got downstairs Smithers was at the bottom and the constables were pounding on the door. I—"

She broke off as a gruff voice called out from the top of the stairs. "Mrs. Parker! If you are finished showing Mrs. Llewellyn the property I should be much obliged if you would assist Winnie in the kitchen."

The housekeeper gave a guilty start and called out, "Be right there!" Turning to Meredith, she added quickly, "I'm sorry, Mrs. Llewellyn. I hope you've seen enough to satisfy you for now?"

Reluctantly, Meredith nodded. She would have liked to have asked a few more questions. Particularly who the housekeeper thought the mysterious visitor might be, but judging from the dark scowl on Smithers's face, she had already overstayed her welcome. She would simply have to wait for another time to find out more about that night.

There was one thing she would very much like to know. Did Smithers know about the visitor's presence in the house that night? If so, why didn't he mention it in his testimony? Those were answers Meredith was most anxious to hear. It appeared that she would have to pay another visit to the Stalham estate in the very near future.

"Now what are we going to do?" Carrying a small sack of potatoes, Grace marched across the kitchen and emptied the sack into the sink. "They've put the village off limits on Saturday. Now you won't be able to hold your protest."

Olivia grunted. "Who won't?" She brought down the knife she was using to chop up a pile of spring greens and smacked it hard on the cutting board. "It's not going to make no difference, so there."

Grace swung around to gape at her. She'd secretly been feeling more than a little relieved at the prospect of postponing the protest, and she didn't like the rebellious look on her friend's face. "Of course it makes a difference! The girls won't go now."

"Who says? We weren't supposed to be protesting anyway, so we would have been breaking the rules. What does it matter if we break one more?"

Grace pinched her lips. "It'll mean a bigger punishment if we're caught, that's what."

"Oh, don't be such a worrywart." Olivia started chopping furiously. "I told you, we won't get caught. No one will even notice we're there, except a few old codgers in the pub, and they're half-blind, anyway."

"What about the people what work there?"

Olivia shrugged. "By the time they realize what's happening, we'll be gone, won't we."

"Not if we stop to smash all the glasses, we won't be."

Olivia uttered a long, tortured sigh. Raising her head, she fastened her dark gaze on Grace's face. "Look, all we are going to do is run through the public bar shouting our slogans. We'll be carrying sticks, and we'll swipe at the glasses as we run past. We'll be out of there before anyone knows what's happening."

Far from reassured, Grace turned back to the sink and picked up the peeling knife. Grabbing a potato out of the water, she began slicing at the skin. "I just bloomin' hope you're right," she muttered. "I'd just like to know why they banned everyone from the village on Saturday."

Olivia paused in her chopping. "No one knows. I asked Mrs. Wilkins and she said she hadn't heard nothing, and I asked Sophie Westchester, 'cos she knows everything, and she said none of the teachers will tell them why. They just told them it was for their own good."

Grace gasped as a thought struck her. "You don't think they heard about the protest, do you, and this is their way of stopping it?"

"Now, how would they find out?"

"Someone might have told them. Someone what didn't want to go and thought the others shouldn't go, neither."

"Nah. Everyone of the girls I asked said they would be there, and they all got sworn into secrecy, so I don't know how anyone would find out. More than likely the teachers don't want the girls joining in the dancing on the green." She put a hand on her hip and in a poor imitation of Mrs. Llewellyn's voice, said haughtily, "Decorum at all times, ladies!"

Grace turned again, the potato still in her hand and dripping cold water down her arm and onto the floor. "But what if someone did tell? Don't you think it would be better to wait until another day to do the protest, when the village isn't banned and we won't get into so much trouble?"

"Saturday is the perfect day. Like I keep telling you, it's May Day and everyone will be out on the green watching the dancing and stuff. That's where the bobby will be, too, so he won't be hanging around the Dog and Duck and the only people what will be there will be the ones too old to dance."

"Well, if everyone will be out on the green, what's the use of protesting in the pub, then, if no one will know we was there?"

"Oh they'll know we was there by the broken glass everywhere. Everyone will be talking about it, wondering who done it and how they got in and out of the village without being caught." Olivia puffed out her scrawny chest. "I think that's really clever to come up with a plan like that."

Grace didn't think it was clever at all. In fact, she still had a really nasty feeling that they were all going to end up in hot water over this one. Still, it looked as if Olivia was bound and determined to go through with it, so she had little say in the matter.

Besides, maybe this time, Olivia was right. It did seem as if they should be able to get in and out of the pub without too many people noticing them. Yeah, this time it was all going to work out and she and Olivia would be heroes for holding a successful protest. With that thought firmly in mind, Grace went back to peeling her potato.

*   *   *

As it was, Meredith was unable to discuss her visit to the Stalham estate with Felicity and Essie until much later that evening. Sylvia had joined them immediately after dinner, much to Felicity's disgust.

"I wish to make a complaint," Sylvia announced, the second she stepped into the teacher's lounge. "Meredith, I must insist you do something about that dastardly assistant of yours."

Meredith exchanged a weary glance with Felicity. "What has Mr. Platt done now?"

Sylvia settled herself on a chair, taking great pains to arrange the folds of her blue linen frock around her ankles. "He has exceeded all boundaries of decency. I caught him in the library, clutching one of the students to his body"—Sylvia shuddered—"while he gyrated with her in the most disgusting manner imaginable." She fanned her face with her hand. "I have never in my life been so utterly shocked and aghast."

Meredith winced. "I do hope you thoroughly chastised him."

"Well, of course I did." Sylvia seemed to be having trouble breathing, and her lisp had become even more prominent as she struggled to get out the words. "I screamed at him to drop the girl at once. He had the *audacity* to tell me he was teaching her the latest dance craze. I ask you, what kind of feeble excuse is that?"

"Were their hands clasped?" Felicity asked, looking amused, which only fueled Sylvia's distress.

"Yes, as a matter of fact, they were." Sylvia frowned. "What does that have to do with anything?"

"He was probably teaching her the tango," Felicity said, disappearing behind the newspaper in her hands.

Sylvia looked as if she would swallow her tongue.

Meredith, deeming it wise to refrain from commenting, shook her head at Essie, who seemed about to join in the fray.

"The *what*?" Sylvia managed at last.

"The tango. It's the latest craze." Felicity leapt from her chair. Holding one hand on her hip and the other in the air, she began humming an outlandish melody with an odd staccato beat and, to everyone's utter astonishment proceeded to swoop all around the floor in what Meredith could only describe as a wanton display of utter indecency.

Chapter 9

Speechless, the other three teachers watched Felicity in openmouthed disbelief, until Meredith finally found her voice. "Felicity Ann Cross, what in heaven's name do you think you are doing?"

Felicity took no notice but continued her provocative prancing until at last, she came to a halt. Twirling her hand in the air, she shouted a breathless, "Olé!"

Essie immediately broke into a burst of applause, while Sylvia sat there, her face set in stone.

"Felicity," Essie cried. "That was marvelous!"

"Wait until you see a man and woman dance it together." Felicity threw herself down on her chair, legs sprawled in front of her. "It will take your breath away."

"Well, *really*." Sylvia tossed her head, sending fronds of her hair floating up and down. "I don't have to sit here and listen to this repulsive discussion."

"No," Felicity agreed mildly. "You don't."

Sylvia gasped, and looked at Meredith for support.

Meredith pretended not to notice. "That was quite an . . . ah . . . energetic dance. What did you call it?"

"The tango." Felicity pulled herself up into a more ladylike posture. "I saw it performed in London last year while I was recruiting a batch of new students. I was in the home of aristocrats, and it was all very respectable. I understand the dance is quite popular in Paris right now, but it hasn't really become well known here. Now yet, anyway." She sent a sly glance in Sylvia's direction. "In fact, I'm surprised Roger Platt is familiar with it."

Sylvia sniffed. "That young man would hunt out the most sordid of behaviors and waste no time in adopting them."

Although Meredith was inclined to agree with her, she felt compelled to defend the wayward assistant. "Oh, come now, Sylvia. If the dance is accepted among London's elite, who are we to condemn it?"

"Indeed." Felicity looked triumphant. "I have to admit, I was intrigued, especially when I learned that it originated in the brothels of Argentina."

"Oh!" Scarlet in the face, Sylvia jumped to her feet. "I adamantly refuse to stay one minute longer and listen to such abominable language."

Felicity raised her eyebrows. "I am speaking nothing but the truth, Sylvia. There are such places, and we can hardly ignore their existence."

"We do not have to mention those dreadful, vulgar places in the drawing room. Good night ladies." With that, Sylvia swept from the room.

"Good. That got rid of her." Felicity rubbed her hands together in glee and the door thudded to a close. "I thought it might."

Meredith shook her head. "You are awful, Felicity. You deliberately provoked her, and with such nonsense, too."

Felicity grinned. "I may have ruffled her feathers, but I assure you, Meredith, everything I said was the truth. I did see the dance performed, and it did originate in Argentina's brothels. The immigrants brought it to Europe and now it's becoming all the rage. It's only a matter of time before it takes London by storm and then everyone will be doing it."

"Not in this school," Meredith said firmly. "If either of you see any of the girls even attempting such a performance, you must put a stop to it at once."

Felicity stared at her. "Didn't you just say we shouldn't condemn the dance if it's accepted by London's aristocracy?"

Meredith tightened her lips. "Accepting it is one thing. Allowing our students to slither all over the halls of this school in that lewd manner is quite something else."

Essie giggled. "It would be quite a sight to see."

Felicity sighed. "Meredith's right. Besides, you really need a man to perform it properly, though why anyone would want to get that close to a male I cannot imagine." She finished her words on a shudder, earning a curious glance from Essie.

Meredith decided now was a good time to change the subject.

Launching into an account of her visit to the Stalham estate, she kept her friends enthralled until she reached the end of her story.

Felicity looked impressed. "You certainly managed to wheedle a great deal of information out of the staff. Well done."

"Except for Smithers, who was the first one on the scene and would therefore have the most specific information." Meredith frowned. "He was quite forbidding, actually. I could tell he resented the intrusion."

"Ah well, you know what butlers can be like." Felicity stretched out her feet and examined the toes of her shoes. "So what did you make of all that?"

"Well, it's apparent that Howard wasn't well liked, though it seems James was well tolerated. I think both the housekeeper and the maid were shocked that he had been convicted of the murder. What really intrigues me, however, is the possible presence of another person in the house that night."

Essie leaned forward. "Do you think there really was someone else in the house when Lord Stalham was shot?"

"I don't know what to think." Meredith smothered a yawn with her hand. "Smithers testified to the opposite. I'd like to hear his side of the story but he's unlikely to tell me." She gave Essie a meaningful look. "On the other hand . . ."

Essie drew back. "Oh, no. Not me. This Smithers person sounds quite intimidating. I just couldn't."

"Oh, bosh, Essie." Felicity leaned over and patted her arm. "Of course you can. You have done it plenty of times before when Meredith has needed information. Looking the way you do, you can wheedle the darkest secrets from the strongest of men. For some strange reason, men simply cannot resist a petite, blond-haired, blue-eyed woman."

A pink glow colored Essie's cheeks. "I'm glad you think I can be of some use."

Felicity laughed. "Oh, come now, Essie. Why so modest? You have a wonderful precious personality that men adore. If you can use it to your advantage, why not?"

Sensing Essie's discomfort, Meredith intervened. "Essie, my dear, Felicity means to compliment you, that's all."

Essie shrugged. "I'm not nearly as clever as you and Felicity in ferreting out the truth."

Meredith smiled. "Essie dear, if it hadn't been for you, I would never have been able to solve anything. You are, indeed, a great help."

"Very well then, if you insist, I shall attempt to talk to the butler." Essie looked down at her hands. "Though I can't guarantee a successful outcome."

"Just as long as you try. That's all I ask." Meredith yawned again. "Dear me. I do believe it's past my bedtime."

"Mine, too." Felicity got to her feet and bent her elbows to stretch her back. "When do you plan to visit the estate again?"

"Tomorrow afternoon, after classes." Meredith tucked her knitting bag back in the drawer and stood. "We can leave Sylvia in charge. I'll tell her we have been invited to a friend's house for a meal."

Essie gasped. "But that means we'll have to go without supper!"

"I'll have a word with Mrs. Wilkins. I'm sure she can arrange something for all of us." Meredith looked at Felicity. "Will that suit you?"

Felicity feigned surprise. "Oh, you want me to come with you?"

"Of course." Meredith crossed to the door. "You surely didn't think I would leave you behind?" She paused and looked back at her. "Of course, you might prefer to stay out of this investigation."

"Oh, I might as well come along. Just to see that the two of you don't end up in trouble."

"Well, then, that's settled." Well pleased, Meredith left the room and headed down the hallway.

Once inside her room, she wasted no time in climbing into bed. As usual, Mrs. Wilkins had left a hot water bottle under the covers, and it was still warm enough to take the chill out of her toes.

Snuggling down under the blankets, Meredith went over the events of the day in her mind. There were still so many unanswered questions. Did Smithers lie on the stand, and if so, why? Was someone else there that night? Was Smithers protecting someone? If so, who? Thinking about it all gave her a headache.

She turned over on her side and pulled the covers up to her chin. As she did so, she thought she saw something move over by the window. Instantly wide awake, she raised her head.

A cold blast of air seemed to wrap itself around her neck.

At the same instant, the pink mist appeared, growing at an alarming rate until it filled the corner of the room.

As the boiling cloud turned red in the middle, Meredith sat up, one hand reaching for the repaired clock at her side. Reggie would not be too pleased if she broke it again, but she felt a little more secure with it clutched in her fingers.

James's face peered out at her from the middle of the mist, his lips moving soundlessly, his eyes staring into space.

Meredith decided to try being civil. "I thought you might return," she said pleasantly.

One arm detached itself from the mist and the fist clenched in the air.

"Yes, I know you're angry. But since I'm not the cause of your pain, I suggest you calm down a little if you want me to help you."

Her words took an instant effect. The arm lowered,

and the dark red swirls began to settle down into a lovely shade of pink.

She could see all of James now, from head to foot. He was dressed in a flowing white robe, and she was startled to see a piece of rope wrapped around his throat. No wonder he was always in a rage.

"I have one question to ask you," she said, beginning to feel a little more secure. "If you tell me the truth, then I will try to find out what really happened the night your father was shot."

The ghost stared back at her, unresponsive.

Meredith took a deep breath. "Did you, or did you not, shoot your father?"

James's mouth opened in a silent roar of outrage. Once more the mist swirled around in deep red spirals, while both arms shot into the air, the clenched fists pounding each other as if in a fierce battle.

Meredith took a firmer grip on the clock. "I'll assume you're protesting your innocence."

For a second or two longer, James's eyes burned with fury, then as quickly as he had appeared, he faded into the mist. The pink swirls swallowed him up, then shrunk into a mere wisp of smoke before vanishing.

Meredith let out her breath. She would have liked to ask him a lot more questions, in spite of the fact he scared her to death. If only her powers were stronger.

Once more she tucked herself under the covers. One thing she could be certain of was that James had every intention of continuing to pester her. Besides, there were just too many questions that needed answering. She was now committed to finding out the truth about Lord Stalham's murder and, perhaps, setting right a grievous miscarriage of justice.

She couldn't give James back his life. All she could
hope for was to clear his name and discover the real culprit. Maybe that would bring the poor man a measure of
peace.

The following day Meredith found the students to be
unusually subdued. Normally they were in high spirits
on a Friday, anticipating the weekend. At first she put it
down to the fact that they had been barred from enjoying
their usual jaunt to the village, and would have to spend
Saturday on the school grounds.

It seemed wherever she went that day, however, small
groups of girls stood about whispering among each other,
only to break off and scatter as she approached. By the
time a rather tense midday meal was over, she felt compelled to voice her concerns to the other tutors.

Sylvia was already in the teacher's lounge when Meredith entered, followed by Felicity and Essie. Meredith
hesitated to mention her misgivings in front of the volatile tutor. Sylvia was apt to panic at the slightest hint of
trouble. Nevertheless, if trouble was indeed brewing, then
Sylvia should certainly be forewarned.

Meredith wasted no time in coming to the point. "I
don't know if any of you have noticed it, but the students
are behaving rather oddly. I have reason to believe they
might have something up their sleeves, though I have no
idea what that may be. Have any of you heard anything
that might possibly shed light on the subject?"

Essie shook her head, while Felicity merely looked
blank.

"I have noticed it, too," Sylvia exclaimed. "I caught a
group of students in the lobby whispering to each other.
The minute I got close to them they all dispersed."

"Precisely." Meredith glanced at the other two tutors.

"Does anyone have any ideas of what they may be whispering about?"

"Not a clue," Felicity said, flopping onto a chair. "I don't pay much attention to them anyway. They are probably planning tango lessons or something." She glanced at Sylvia, and was rewarded with a scowl.

"Well, I suppose we shall find out in due course." Meredith sat down next to her. "I don't think they can get into too much trouble, since they will be confined to the school for the entire weekend."

"Except for when we go to church on Sunday," Sylvia reminded her with a slightly accusing air.

"Of course." Meredith curbed a sigh. "I did feel, however, that I should warn you all to be on your guard. The more prepared we are for trouble, the more likely we'll be able to take care of it." Bracing herself, she added, "Which brings me to a favor I must ask of you, Sylvia."

The tutor turned her head, her expression wary. "I certainly hope you're not expecting me to watch over these girls all by myself."

Ignoring Essie's gasp of dismay, Meredith smiled. "Only for a short while. Felicity, Essie, and I have been invited to a friend's house for supper. The students will all be in their rooms or in the library. I shall ask Mr. Platt to remain here until we return. He will assist you should anything untoward happen."

Sylvia's face registered stark horror. "I can't possibly rely on that young man! Why, he is usually the one to instigate trouble. You must know that."

"Please don't fret about it. I'll have a word with him before I leave."

"I really don't think—" Sylvia began, but Meredith cut in with a raised hand.

"It's all settled, Sylvia. I trust that you will rise to the occasion with your usual competence and fortitude. I have every confidence in your ability to handle whatever problem may arise."

"Well, I fully intend to speak to Mr. Hamilton about all this on his next visit." Sylvia marched to the door, her chin jutting out in defiance. "He should know that your assistant is nothing but an insufferable troublemaker."

"I do believe he's aware of that," Meredith murmured, but her answer was lost in the slamming of the door.

"Ouch." Felicity winced. "I have an idea Miss Montrose is a little miffed about something."

"Nothing more than I expected." Meredith sat down on the nearest chair. "It can't be helped. I need both of you to come with me if we are to get to the bottom of this murder."

Felicity gave her a look full of curiosity. "You certainly seem dedicated to the cause."

"I am." Meredith paused, then added quietly, "James came to visit me again last night."

Essie gasped, her hand covering her mouth.

"Oh, here we go again." Felicity shook her head. "What did he tell you this time?"

Meredith gave her a withering look. "You know quite well he can't speak to me. I asked if he had killed his father."

Glancing at the clock, she rose to her feet. "He made it quite clear by his actions that he was outraged at the question. We must leave. Reggie should have the carriage at the front steps by now."

Felicity sighed and climbed to her feet. "Then let's get this over with before I faint from hunger."

Meredith rolled her eyes. "We shall be back here soon

after our normal supper time. Mrs. Wilkins has promised to have soup and sandwiches waiting for us in the kitchen when we return."

"Then lead on." Felicity stomped across the room and opened the door. "Our enemies await."

Essie looked startled. "Our enemies?"

"Just a phrase, that's all." Felicity walked out into the hallway, and Essie, seeming only partly reassured, followed her.

Meredith stepped out after them and closed the door. Although she refrained from saying as much, she couldn't help wondering if perhaps Felicity's words might prove prophetic. She had seen something in the aloof butler's eyes that had made her most uneasy, and she could only hope that she wasn't leading them all into jeopardy.

Chapter 10

Some time later, as they all marched up the steps of the Stalhams' mansion to the tune of the barking dogs, Meredith still harbored a feeling of apprehension. She had prepared her speech and was well versed in what she would say. Even so, when the door opened to reveal the steely-eyed butler, the skin on her arms prickled.

"Good afternoon." She smiled, though her lips felt stiff and unresponsive. "I was so enchanted with this beautiful estate I brought my sister, Miss Felicity Cross, to look at it. I trust her opinion, and I just know she is going to simply love it, as I do."

Smithers looked at her as if she'd just crawled out from under a stone. "You have an appointment?"

Meredith was about to answer when Felicity stepped forward.

"We are here to decide whether or not we wish to purchase this property. Please inform your superiors that we wish to look around."

"I *am* the superior here." Smithers's eyes burned with resentment. Meredith almost expected steam to rise from his head.

Felicity looked him up and down. "Really. Well in that case, my good man, you will have no objection if we come in." Without waiting for him to answer, she stepped over the threshold, forcing the butler to retreat.

Glancing over her shoulder, she signaled with her eyes for Meredith to follow. Essie seemed frozen to the spot. Meredith took hold of her arm and propelled her forward, then followed her into the vast entrance.

Smithers fixed his menacing stare on Essie. "And pray, who is this?"

"Oh," Meredith said hurriedly, "this is . . . ah . . . my niece. Miss Esmeralda Pickard."

Essie still wore that petrified expression, and Felicity gave her a hearty nudge with her elbow. "Smile, child. Remember your manners."

Essie drew her lips back over her teeth. "Pleased to make your acquaintance," she murmured.

The butler's gaze lingered for a moment longer on her face, then traveled back to Meredith. "I will see if Mrs. Parker is available."

"Please do so," Felicity said cheerfully.

Smithers dismissed her with another of his chilling glances and stalked off down the hallway.

"Hmmph!" Felicity muttered. "He's a bit of a snob if you ask me."

"He scares me." Essie shivered. "I don't think he'll even talk to us, much less tell us anything."

"He'll talk to you." Felicity gave her an encouraging smile. "Just bat your eyelashes at him and flash those dimples. He'll be bleating like a lamb in no time."

Meredith had to laugh. "I'm afraid Essie might be right. I can't see that man melting in the face of the sun. But it's worth a try."

Essie frowned. "Well, if you say so, but I really don't think it will do any good."

The sound of footsteps turned her head, and Meredith followed her gaze. Mrs. Parker was hurrying toward them, her face creased in anxiety.

"Mr. Smithers asked me to be as quick as possible," she said, when she reached them. "So if you'll come this way, Mrs. Llewellyn, I'll take you to the drawing room."

Following the housekeeper down the hallway, Meredith leaned closer to Essie. "At the first opportunity, slip away and try to find Smithers. You know what to ask him."

Essie nodded as Mrs. Parker paused in front of a pair of large doors. Throwing them open, she announced, "This is the drawing room. It was recently renovated, as you can see by the embossed wallpaper and satin curtains. The carpet is an Oriental, sent over from China, and is largely silk."

Apparently Lady Clara favored flamboyance in her furnishings, Meredith thought, as she gazed upon the dazzling colors of the red, green, and yellow carpet. She had to admit, it was rather striking. Not to her taste, however. She preferred something a little more subdued.

Mrs. Parker had walked over to the windows and was tugging at the curtains to open them. Meredith glanced over at Essie and nodded. The young teacher nodded back, then quietly slipped out into the hallway and disappeared.

Having won her battle with the curtains, Mrs. Parker turned. "As you can see—" She broke off, staring around the room. "Your niece! Where is she?"

Meredith looked around as if noticing Essie's absence for the first time. "She isn't here? Oh, she is probably looking around on her own. She's rather independent, I'm afraid."

The housekeeper passed a worried hand over her hair. "Oh, dear, oh, dear, Mr. Smithers won't like that at all. He's very strict about who's allowed in the house."

"I'm sure she will cause no harm." Meredith looked at Felicity. "So what do you think of this room? Do you think it would suit us?"

Felicity creased her brow in a thoughtful expression. "It's very grand, to be sure. I'd need to see more of the house, however, before passing on my opinion."

"I'll be happy to show you the library." Mrs. Parker crossed the garish carpet to the door. "Though Mrs. Lewellyn has already seen it."

"I would like my sister to see it, too," Meredith said, giving Felicity a meaningful look.

"Oh, is that the room where the late Lord Stalham was shot? Felicity followed the housekeeper out into the hallway. "My sister told me all about it. What a terrible tragedy. It must have caused a tremendous upheaval in the house."

"Oh, it did, indeed." Mrs. Parker opened the door to the library and led them inside. "As I told your sister, it upset everyone."

"A terrible shock," Meredith said, addressing Felicity. "Mrs. Parker told me everyone in the house was asleep when it happened."

"That we were." The housekeeper shook her head. "The minute I heard the dogs barking that night, I knew something was wrong. They were barking at the constables, of course. That's what woke me up."

Meredith stood in the middle of the room, while Felicity wandered about, finally coming to a halt in front of the gun cabinet. "Which one of these is the gun that killed Lord Stalham?"

Meredith held her breath at her friend's audacity, but the housekeeper seemed ready to answer as she hurried over there.

"That one," she said, pointing at it. "They say it used to belong to Jesse James, the American bank robber, though I don't know how true that is."

"Really." Felicity leaned closer to get a better look. "It certainly must have put quite a hole in him. It looks really heavy."

This time Mrs. Parker seemed at a loss for words, and Meredith hurriedly intervened. "We heard the dogs when we walked up the steps earlier," she said, sending Felicity a warning scowl.

"Oh, they bark at everyone, coming and going." Abandoning Felicity, the housekeeper drew closer to Meredith. "That's how I knew someone else was in the house that night. I heard them barking earlier in the evening. Twice. So someone must have came and went before I went to bed."

"Before the constables arrived, you mean?"

Mrs. Parker nodded. "Oh, yes. Quite a while before that. I was in my room reading at the time. Then I got ready for bed, and I'd been asleep for a while after that when the dogs woke me up again." She shook her head. "Making such a racket, they were. Like I said, I knew at once something was wrong. I fell out of bed, threw on my dressing gown, and rushed right down the stairs."

"Did you see him?" Felicity came forward, her face alight with interest. "The dead body, I mean."

"Oh, no." Mrs. Parker shuddered. "Mr. Smithers met me at the bottom of the stairs. Told me the master had been shot and to go back to my room. I was that upset I did exactly what he said."

"Did anyone else come down with you?" Meredith asked, as Felicity wandered over to the fireplace.

"Winnie was in the hallway when I came down. Her room is next to mine at the front of the house. The other maids all sleep in the back."

"Do you have any idea who the dogs might have been barking at earlier?"

The housekeeper hesitated, obviously burning to tell Meredith something yet wary of saying too much. Finally, her gossiping nature got the better of her. "Well, I don't know for sure, of course, and even if I did, it's not my place to say, but . . ." Her voice trailed off as she waited for reassurance from Meredith.

"I swear we won't repeat anything you tell us," Meredith promised. "I'm just curious, that's all. If I'm to buy this estate I'd really like to know what happened here that night. It's the not knowing that's so worrisome. One tends to imagine all sorts of things."

"Of course." Seemingly satisfied, the housekeeper looked around as if she expected someone else to be in the room. "Well, like I said, I can't be sure of anything. But Jimmy, the new stable lad, told me he heard horse's hooves that night. He lives over the stables, you see, so he'd be able to hear if one came into the courtyard. Only no one summoned him to take care of it, so he didn't bother going down."

"Did he see who it was?"

Meredith held her breath as the housekeeper hesitated once more. Finally she lowered her voice to a whisper.

"He said he peeked out the window and only saw her face for an instant, but he thinks it was a friend of Lord Howard's, Miss Pauline Suchier."

Across the room Felicity uttered a quiet gasp. The housekeeper looked at her in surprise and Felicity quickly picked up a figurine from the mantelpiece. "Exquisite," she murmured. "Simply exquisite."

Mrs. Parker's eyes narrowed. "You are acquainted with Miss Suchier?"

"Oh, not at all," Meredith said quickly. "We have never heard of the lady."

Mrs. Parker sniffed. "I don't know so much about her being a lady. She was the reason Lord Howard came down here on the weekends. Without his wife, if you get my meaning." She sent Meredith a sly look. "Though I did hear as how the master was planning on getting rid of her. Miss Suchier, I mean. Mr. Smithers happened to hear a conversation between Lord Howard and James, and Smithers said we wouldn't be seeing much of her in the future. I—" The door opened just then, cutting off whatever she was going to say next.

Essie sailed into the room, her smile letting Meredith know that she'd managed to learn something from the dour butler.

Dying to know what he had to say, Meredith said quickly, "Well, thank you, Mrs. Parker. I think we've seen enough for now. Though we might be back again for another look around in a day or two."

The housekeeper nodded. "By all means, Mrs. Llewellyn. There's not a lot to do nowadays, except keep the place clean and tidy and feed the staff. What's left of them. We haven't had anyone else even look at the place besides you. Makes a nice change to get out of the kitchen. I must say, I'll be really pleased once it's sold and I can go back to London."

Felicity looked surprised. "You don't like living in this grand house?"

"No, I don't. Too quiet for me." The housekeeper rubbed her arms as if she were cold. "This place gives me the willies now. I keep thinking I can see James walking around. He loved to play tricks, especially on poor Winnie. Used to creep up behind her and shout in her ear. It's a wonder she hasn't dropped dead of a heart attack before now. Sometimes I think I can still see him creeping along the hallways."

Felicity exchanged a look with Meredith, while Essie clutched her upper arms and sent a frightened glance around the room.

"Well, we won't take up any more of your time." Meredith followed the scrawny woman to the door. "Thank you so much for showing us around. We'll see ourselves out."

The housekeeper appeared relieved. "Oh, would you? I know Mr. Smithers will be looking for me by now." She hurried off, leaving the teachers alone.

"Certainly." Out in the hallway, Meredith caught sight of Winnie hurrying down the stairs. "Both of you go on without me," she said quickly, her voice hushed. "I'd like a quick word with the maid. I'll catch up with you on the steps."

Essie looked as if she was happy to get out of the mansion, though Felicity seemed reluctant to leave. Nevertheless, she followed Essie to the front door, while Meredith waited at the foot of the stairs.

Winnie's footsteps slowed as she approached Meredith, until she finally halted on the bottom stair. Dropping a slight curtsey, she mumbled, "Is there something I can do for you, Mrs. Llewellyn?"

"I just wanted a word with you." Meredith smiled in an attempt to put the girl at ease. "Mrs. Parker believes someone else was in the house the night of the shooting, despite what Smithers said on the stand. I was just wondering if you happened to see anyone here that night."

Winnie looked as if she wanted to flee down the hallway. "I didn't see nothing."

Meredith looked into the frightened girl's eyes. "Winnie, I think there's a strong possibility that James Stalham might not be the person who shot Lord Howard. If that's so, I think it's only right that the real killer is found and punished, don't you? If there's anything at all that you can tell me that might help find this person, I'd very much like to hear it."

Winnie's bottom lip trembled, and tears formed in her eyes. "I did see someone," she whispered. "Right before the constables arrived. At least, I think I did. I'm not exactly sure, which is why I didn't say nothing before, but I think I saw her running down the back steps to the kitchen."

Meredith felt a surge of triumph. "Who was it, Winnie? You can tell me. I promise you won't get into trouble for it."

Winnie gulped, then whispered again. "Well, I don't know what she was doing on the kitchen stairs, I swear I don't, but I thought I recognized her cloak and hat. I think I saw Lady Clara, m'm."

Meredith stared at her for a moment, then nodded. "Thank you, Winnie."

The maid looked about to say something else, then apparently thought better of it. Instead, she ducked her head, then ran down the hallway and out of sight.

Hurrying out of the front doors, Meredith found Felicity and Essie waiting for her at the top of the steps. Amid a barrage of furious barking from the dogs, she raised her voice. "Well, Essie, did Smithers tell you anything?"

Essie danced down the steps, forcing Meredith to hurry after her in order to hear what she had to say. "He didn't tell me much," she said, when they reached the bottom. "He's not very good at holding a conversation."

Above them, Felicity let out a short burst of laughter. "I doubt if he knows how. I knew if anyone could get him to talk, though, it would be you. You're a positive genius when it comes to worming information out of someone."

Essie blushed. "I just ask questions, and hope I'll get some answers, that's all."

"Ah, but it's in the way you ask them." Felicity marched down the steps. "You are a born coquette, Essie dear, and your charm is in the fact that you have absolutely no idea of the disarming effect you have on the male population."

Essie pouted. "You make me sound like a harlot."

"Do I? I certainly don't mean to offend."

Having run out of patience, Meredith grasped Essie's arm. "I refuse to let you go another step until you've told me what Smithers told you."

"Oh, I'm sorry." Essie gave her an apologetic smile. "Well, he told me he heard the shot and rushed to the library, where he found Lord Stalham lying on the carpet and James standing over him, holding the gun. He's absolutely certain James killed his father. Smithers said anyone else would not have had time to leave before he got there. In any case, he said, the dogs would have barked if anyone had come close to the house, and the only time he heard the dogs barking was when the constables arrived, and again when they left with James."

Meredith wrinkled her brow. "That's not what Mrs. Parker told us. She said she heard them barking before the constables arrived."

"Twice," Felicity said, nodding her head.

Essie looked surprised. "Why would Smithers lie about that?"

"I've been thinking about that," Meredith murmured. "He also lied about Miss Suchier's relationship with Lord Stalham. I believe he might have been protecting someone."

She started walking away from the mansion's steps with Felicity hot on her heels. "Protecting who? That Suchier woman? Was that why he lied about her?"

"No, not Pauline Suchier." Meredith paused again. "Winnie told me she thought she saw Lady Clara that night, running down the back stairs to the kitchen. I think both lies were to protect her."

Felicity's eyes widened. "Oh, my. That complicates things, doesn't it."

"What complicates things?" Essie asked, catching up with them.

Meredith told her about Winnie's revelation. "You know," she added, as they all began walking again, "Mrs. Parker could be lying, of course. Also to protect Lady Clara. She took care to let us know the stable boy saw Pauline Suchier that night."

"Or thought he did," Felicity put in. "He could have been mistaken. After all, didn't he say he only saw her face for an instant?"

"I need to have a word with him." Meredith nodded her head at the side of the building. "I believe Reggie took the carriage around to the stables to wait for us. While you and Essie are getting into the carriage, I'll see if I can spot the stable boy and ask him a question or two. Perhaps we'll learn something useful from him."

"I hope so." Felicity frowned. "So far everything we've heard has only raised more questions."

" I tell you, Meredith," Essie put in, "your ghost is not going to cross over, or whatever it's called, unless you can find someone who really knows what happened in the library that night."

"You're right." Meredith sighed. "But I'm afraid that the only one who knows what really happened is the person who shot Lord Stalham, and something tells me that person is not about to come up to me and confess."

Essie gave her a worried smile. "I do fear that you might be haunted by James forever."

Chapter 11

Meredith led the way around the corner to where Reggie had left the carriage. Spirit tossed his head impatiently as she approached, but she could see no sign of Reggie. "He must be in the stables," she said as Felicity and Essie joined her. "That will give me an excuse to talk to the stable boy. Both of you wait here for me. I shan't be long."

"Why can't we come along?"

Essie pouted, and Felicity nudged her with her elbow. "Do you really want to go in that nasty, smelly place, with your skirts sweeping through God knows what hidden in the filthy straw?"

Essie's frown disappeared. "Well, now that you mention it, I think I'll wait in here." With a nod at Meredith she lifted her skirts and stepped up into the carriage.

"I didn't think so." Looking smug, Felicity added, "Try not to be too long. I'm starving to death."

"I'll be as fast as I can." Holding up the hem of her own skirt, Meredith hurried toward the stable.

Just as she got there, Reggie appeared in the entrance, looking flustered. "Sorry, m'm. Didn't realize you were done talking, did I. I'll be right along."

"That's all right, Reggie." Meredith smiled. "I just want a quick word with the stable boy. Is he in there?"

Reggie turned his head and glanced behind him. "What, Jimmy? No, he's not . . ."

His voice trailed off as a tall, lanky lad strolled out into the sunshine. "Someone asking for me?"

Reggie looked even more flustered. The reason was obvious, since Jimmy held a pack of playing cards in one hand, and some pound notes in the other. "Oh, you are there, then." Reggie looked back at Meredith with a sickly grin. "Didn't see him there in the glare of the sun."

Meredith decided the question of Reggie's gambling could be postponed. "Wait for me in the carriage," she ordered.

With a last look at Jimmy, Reggie bolted across the yard.

"My name is Mrs. Llewellyn," Meredith began, and Jimmy nodded.

"Yes, I know. Reggie told me all about you."

"Oh?" Though sorely tempted, Meredith decided that it might be wiser not to ask. "Well, I was wondering if you could tell me about the night Lord Stalham was shot."

Jimmy looked over his shoulder, then frowned at her. "Why should I, if you don't mind me asking?"

Again Meredith wondered just what Reggie had told the young man. She'd had to rely on her maintenance man's discretion more than once, and Reggie had been sworn to secrecy about her activities concerning certain nefarious events. Just how far she could trust him remained to be seen.

"Let us just say I have a vested interest in what happened that night."

Jimmy's brow wrinkled even further. "Vested?"

Meredith sighed. She hated the falsehood she had perpetrated, but it seemed she had no choice. She could only hope the end justified the means. "I'm thinking of purchasing this property, and I'd rather there weren't any secrets about this place."

Jimmy's brow cleared. "Oh, well, it ain't no secret, m'm. It were all in the newspaper so I don't see no harm in speaking up about it now. Lord Stalham, James, that is—he was a lord such a short time it don't seem right to call him one. He didn't become a lord, you see, until his father died, and then he died himself shortly afterward so it were sort of wasted on him, weren't it. Now his father, that was a different matter. Everyone called him Lord Stalham, which is why it were hard to call James that, 'cos we were so used to—"

"You were going to tell me about that night," Meredith cut in, a little desperately. It seemed that Jimmy liked the sound of his own voice, and his steady stream of words seemed unstoppable.

Jimmy looked offended. "Well, I was just coming to that, wasn't I. It was like this. I was half asleep, upstairs on me bed, when I heard the sound of horse hooves. The dogs started barking and carrying on and I thought, blimey, who's this coming in here so bleeding late at night?" He slapped a hand over his mouth. "Sorry, m'm. Didn't mean to swear. It just sort of slipped out, it did."

"That's quite all right, Jimmy," Meredith murmured. "Please, do go on."

"Yes, well." Jimmy tucked the pound notes into his

back pocket then, without even looking at them, he started flipping the cards back and forth through his fingers.

No wonder Reggie lost his money, Meredith thought. He should have known better. This young man was obviously an expert with the playing cards.

"Well," Jimmy said, "at first I thought I'd pretend I didn't hear anything so as I could go back to sleep. I was comfortable, you see, and I didn't want to have to get up and get dressed and go downstairs and stable the horse and than have to wait for whoever it was to be done with their business, and then I'd just get settled again and I'd have to go down and get the horse out again and see them off before I could go back to bed. It didn't make no sense to me at all. I mean, I'd been working all day and—"

"So then you must have changed your mind," Meredith said firmly.

Jimmy clamped his mouth shut and for a moment she was afraid he wouldn't say anything else. She was about to apologize for interrupting when he said abruptly, "Well, yes, I did. I got up and looked out of the window."

Meredith let out her breath. "Did you recognize the visitor?"

Jimmy hesitated, and she could tell he was keeping her in suspense, no doubt to punish her for being so impatient with him.

At long last, just as she was ready to give up, he muttered, "Well, I could see she was a woman. She was walking fast and by the time I looked out she was at the corner of the house."

"But did you recognize her?"

Jimmy shrugged. "Well, it were dark, weren't it, with only a sliver of a moon. Didn't give out too much light. You need a full moon to see properly across this yard.

Besides, she were quite far away and she had her back to me. It was really hard to see from here."

With a supreme effort Meredith held on to her tongue and waited.

Finally Jimmy relented. "Then, just as the lady reached the corner, she turned sideways and the moon lit up her face. Her hat put part of it in shadow, but I saw enough to recognize her. It were Miss Pauline Suchier. Lord Howard's paramour, so they say."

"I see." Meredith strained to keep the triumph out of her voice. "Did you see her leave?"

Jimmy's eyebrows lifted. "Leave? No, I didn't." He looked thoughtful for a moment. "I heard the bobbies come, and then I heard them leave again with Lord Stalham—James, that is. But I don't remember hearing Miss Suchier leave. Though her horse was gone when I went down to see what all the fuss was about with the bobbies. I must have been asleep when she left."

"Well, thank you, Jimmy. You have been most helpful." Meredith turned away, but Jimmy's next words halted her.

"Did you by any chance talk to Mrs. Parker about what happened that night?"

"Yes, I did." She looked over her shoulder at him. "Why do you ask?"

Jimmy shrugged. "I was just wondering, that's all. She wasn't exactly cut up over the master's death, you know. Lord Howard Stalham, that is."

Very slowly, Meredith twisted around to face him. "Mrs. Parker disliked Lord Stalham?"

Jimmy made a face. "Not disliked, m'm. Hated him, she did. For what he did to her son."

"Her son?"

"Yes, m'm. Her son, Edward. He was the stable lad

before me. Lord Stalham gave him a terrible beating one day. It took Edward three days before he could walk and the minute he got on his feet he scarpered."

Meredith frowned. "Scarpered?"

Jimmy nodded. "Vamoosed. You know. Ran away. I don't think Mrs. Parker will ever forget that."

Casting her mind back, Meredith recalled her conversation with the housekeeper. Of course. She should have realized. Mrs. Parker had said that the stable boy *still* had the scars of that beating. How would she know that, months later, unless she had seen him? Why didn't she mention that he was her son?

Meredith sighed. There were more twists and turns to this mystery than she could fathom. After thanking Jimmy again, she made her way over to the carriage, where Felicity and Essie waited for her. Reggie sat on his seat in the carriage, reins in his hand.

"I was just coming to look for you," Felicity said, her voice short with impatience. "Essie and I are just about ready to faint from hunger."

"I could use something to eat meself," Reggie put in, as he jumped down to open the carriage door. "How about us all going down to the Dog and Duck for a pint and a sandwich?"

Felicity's eyes lit up, but Meredith shook her head. "Mrs. Wilkins has supper ready for us in the kitchen," she said, as she climbed up onto her seat. "We can't possibly let such good food go to waste."

"Right ho. Perhaps another time." With a cheerful grin, Reggie slammed the door.

"Does he know why we are visiting the estate?" Felicity asked in a whisper. "He hasn't asked, but he must wonder what we are doing here."

"I've just told him we're looking over the property, but I think he's guessed I'm working on an investigation." Meredith settled her back against the seat with another sigh. It had been a long day.

Felicity gave her a sharp look. "Are you quite sure that's wise?"

"He's fully aware that now and then, I have reason to make enquiries about certain . . . ah . . . delicate matters. He's always been quite willing to go along without asking too many questions. If you remember, he was most helpful the last time we were involved in similar circumstances."

"Well, then, tell us what you found out from the stable boy."

Meredith recounted everything she'd learned.

"Lord Howard sounds like an ogre," Essie said, "though we shouldn't speak ill of the dead. Still, it seems there were a lot of people who had reason to despise him."

"It does indeed," Meredith agreed.

"So, there *were* two visitors there that night." Felicity's eyes sparkled with intrigue. "The paramour and the wife. How very interesting."

Meredith frowned. "Mrs. Parker, however, insisted the dogs barked only twice before the constables arrived, which would mean only one person came and went."

"That's right." Felicity shook her head. "So if Mrs. Parker is telling the truth, either Winnie or Jimmy must have been mistaken. On the other hand, perhaps both Jimmy and Winnie were telling the truth and *both* Lady Clara and Miss Suchier were there. Mrs. Parker could have slept through the dogs barking, just like the stable boy did."

"Or," Meredith said slowly, "supposing Miss Suchier left at the same time Lady Clara arrived, which was the second time the dogs barked, and then Lady Clara left when the constables arrived? Winnie said she saw Lady Clara just before the constables got there."

Felicity thought about it, while Essie sat with a confused frown on her face. "That would work," Felicity announced at last. "In which case, both Winnie and Jimmy would be right. If that's so, I wonder if Lady Clara saw Miss Suchier leaving the premises and realized that her husband was engaged in a little hanky-panky."

"It's possible. It would certainly give her a motive for shooting her husband."

Felicity nodded. "As William Congreve said in his immortal words, 'Heaven has no rage like love to hatred turned, nor hell a fury like a woman scorned.'"

"Precisely. I do feel that either Miss Suchier or Lady Clara could have shot Lord Stalham. Since both of them would certainly have been wearing gloves, that would have eliminated the need to clean the gun and presumably given either one of them time to leave the room before Smithers arrived."

Essie gasped, while Felicity chuckled. "Well done, Meredith. It makes perfect sense. The killer could certainly have been wearing gloves when she took hold of the gun, and the only people likely to be wearing them would be those two ladies. You are quite getting the hang of this detective business, aren't you."

Meredith shook her head. "There are no real conclusions to all this, just a lot of guesses and possibilities. I don't know how Inspector Dawson does this for a living. All this brainstorming gives me quite a headache."

"There's just one thing," Essie said, surprising her friends. "I have never met Lady Clara, of course, but would a mother allow her own son to die to cover up her own sins? I would think she would have to be an extraordinarily cruel and heartless woman to do such a terrible thing."

Both Meredith and Felicity stared at Essie. Then Felicity broke the silence with another soft chuckle. "She certainly has a point there."

"Yes, she does." Meredith brightened. "In which case, it seems the most likely suspect is Miss Suchier. If you remember, Mrs. Parker mentioned that Lord Howard had planned to be rid of her."

"The woman scorned again," Felicity murmured. "There's just one thing. How do you prove it?"

Meredith passed a hand across her forehead. "I have no idea. Are you feeling as confused as I am?"

"Probably." Felicity sat back, shaking her head. "It's too bad your ghost just can't tell you who killed his father."

"Even if he could, I wouldn't be able hear him. He's tried once or twice to tell me something, but I suppose my powers don't stretch that far. It's all very frustrating."

"Can't you just read his lips? You certainly have a talent for that," Essie said, straightening her hat, which had slipped sideways at the last bump in the road.

Meredith frowned. "That's another strange thing. For some reason, although I can see his lips moving, I can't see what he's saying."

"Even though he's in the same room?" Essie looked incredulous. "That *is* strange. I've seen you read someone's lips from twenty yards away."

Meredith sighed. "Well, in any case, I don't think James knows who killed his father. After all, if he was telling the truth, he arrived in the library to find his father shot and the killer gone."

"Oh, that's right. I'd forgotten that." Felicity glanced out the window as the carriage swayed violently on its way around a sharp curve.

Meredith grabbed her hat. "We shall simply have to work all this out for ourselves, though I can't help feeling that somewhere in all that confusing information lies the answer to all our questions."

"Well, if so, I hope you discover it soon." Felicity looked disgruntled. "If Hamilton learns what you are up to, and that we're assisting you, there'll be hell to pay."

Essie gasped. "I do hope he doesn't find out."

"He hasn't so far," Meredith said crisply, "and I don't see any reason why he would this time."

"What about Sylvia? She certainly has her suspicions." Felicity grabbed onto the window ledge as the carriage again rocked from side to side. "Drat that Reggie. He takes the corners much too fast."

Meredith swayed to one side and righted herself. "Sylvia won't find out either as long as we don't talk about this in her presence."

"Absolutely right. Only we're telling so many lies lately, we're bound to be caught out in one sooner or later."

Meredith frowned. "I don't like to think of it as lying. I prefer to think that we are fabricating excuses for our absence, in the interest of all parties concerned."

Felicity grinned. "Well put. Nevertheless, if our excuses are exposed as untrue, we shall still be in trouble."

"Then we shall just have to face the music if that happens." Meredith settled herself more firmly on the seat. "Meanwhile, if this is the only way I can be rid of these pesky ghosts who insist on haunting me, then I shall do my utmost to resolve whatever it is keeping them here.

Now, let us move on to more pleasant things. Essie, tell us, how are your classes coming along?"

To her relief, Essie seized the opportunity to relate a story about a group of her students who thought it would be funny to arrive in class wearing their sleeping attire. "I made them lie on the floor as if they were in bed for the entire class," she said, making Felicity chuckle again. "I don't think they will be so eager to pull such a trick again."

Meredith listened with half an ear as Felicity answered with an anecdote of her own. Something that Winnie had told her kept coming back to tease her mind. Something important. Now, if only she could remember what it was, she might be a little closer to solving this entire frustrating puzzle.

Chapter 12

"So," Olivia said, as she followed Grace to the dining room, "you remember everything you have to do tomorrow, I hope? You haven't forgotten what I said?"

"Of course I remember." Grace balanced her heavy tray on her hip and shoved her cap higher up her forehead. "It's not hard, is it. I follow you and the girls into the pub and smash all the glasses I can get my hands on before we all run out again."

"That's right." Olivia grunted as she hoisted her own tray higher. "Once we get to the pub I need you to bring up the rear so you can make sure we don't have any stragglers."

In spite of her anxiety, Grace had to smile. "Bring up the rear? You sound just like that Christabel Pankhurst that led the protest in Witcheston."

"Well, that's what I am, too, aren't I. A blooming suffragette." Olivia halted as Grace aimed a kick at the door of the dining room. "Wait a minute. Listen to that. What the blooming heck is all that noise?"

Grace winced as the door swung back and smacked against the wall. Not that it mattered, because any sound she had made was drowned out by the uproar inside the room. Her ears rang with the clamor of crashing dishes and strident voices.

At one end of the farthest table, a savage food fight was in progress, with carrots, mashed potatoes, and buns flying back and forth. Every now and then a shriek erupted when a missile found its mark.

Students stood on top of the other three tables, cheering and stomping their feet, making the plates dance and rattle until some of them slid off the edge of the table and crashed to the floor.

Close by, a larger group of students stood with locked arms, chanting, "We'll smash their glasses, and put 'em on their arses. Equal rights for women!"

In the midst of it all, Miss Montrose leapt up and down like a frenzied frog, arms waving, screaming at the top of her voice, her words lost in the tumult of noise all around her.

"Bloody hell," Olivia yelled in Grace's ear, "what's going on?"

Grace looked around, but could see no sign of any of the other teachers. Leaning close to Olivia, she yelled back. "It looks like Miss Montrose is all by herself and doesn't know how to take charge."

Olivia shook her head, then marched to the nearest table and slammed her tray down on the end of it. A currant bun sailed through the air and narrowly missed her ear. Olivia promptly picked up the tray, walked over to the nearest student and hit her over the head with it.

The student sat down rather suddenly, and Grace winced. That had to hurt. The girl next to her turned on

Olivia and raised her hand to slap her. The maid calmly grabbed her wrist and gave it a hefty twist. The student screamed, and everyone around her stopped shouting and turned to see what all the yelling was about.

Just then, the door burst open and Roger Platt came rushing in. Sylvia Montrose took one look at him and burst into tears.

It took a moment for Grace to realize why, but then she saw another figure fill the doorway. It was Stuart Hamilton, and the look on his face was enough to turn back a herd of rampaging elephants.

"It's very quiet," Felicity observed, as she led the way through the door into the school lobby. "The girls must be all safely tucked up in their rooms. Looks as though Sylvia managed to take care of everything."

Meredith frowned as they passed by the library. Looking through the window at all the empty tables, she muttered, "Something's wrong. It's far too early for the students to have retired for the night."

"Perhaps they're still in the dining room, having a late meal. I'll go and see." Essie started in that direction, then halted as the tall figure of Stuart Hamilton strode purposefully toward them.

"Uh-oh," Felicity murmured. "It would seem the lord and master is displeased."

Meredith felt a thump of apprehension. Ignoring Felicity's sarcasm, she hurried forward. "Mr. Hamilton? Is something wrong?"

Hamilton halted and crossed his arms. "Why on earth would you possibly imagine that anything could be wrong?"

As always, his piercing gaze seemed to bore right through her head. "I . . . ah . . . don't know. It's just that it seems so quiet and . . ."

"We're wondering where the students are," Felicity said at her side.

"We thought perhaps they might still be in the dining room," Essie said timidly, as she sidled up on the other side of Meredith.

Hamilton transferred his gaze to the young tutor. "I can assure you, they are not in the dining room," he said, his words edged in ice.

Certain now of some dire disaster, Meredith swallowed. "I . . . ah . . . perhaps you could tell us where they are?"

"They are all confined to their rooms. For the entire weekend." Hamilton unfolded his arms and tucked a thumb in his trousers pocket. "No doubt you are agog with curiosity to learn why such a drastic move was necessary."

Meredith raised her chin. "Whatever it is, I'm quite sure Miss Montrose had good reason to discipline the students and will no doubt explain. If I'm allowed the opportunity to speak with her, that is."

A glint appeared in Hamilton's eyes. "Miss Montrose," he said heavily, "did not send the students to their rooms. I did. Miss Montrose is, at this moment, indulging in a fit of hysterics in the teacher's lounge."

"Well, good for her," Felicity murmured.

Grasping at the remnants of her composure, Meredith turned to Essie. "Please go to the teacher's lounge and see if you can do anything for Miss Montrose. Felicity, I'd appreciate it if you could look in on the students and make sure all is well with them."

Essie scuttled off with a look of relief on her face, while Felicity hesitated. "Are you certain you want to handle this on your own?"

"Quite certain."

"Very well." She shot a glowering look at Hamilton before stalking off.

Meredith waited until Felicity's long stride had taken her out of earshot before addressing Hamilton once more. "Perhaps if we can retire to my office, where we can speak with more privacy?"

"By all means." He gave her a deep, mocking bow. "Do, please, lead the way."

Gritting her teeth, she set off down the corridor. To her embarrassment, her stomach uttered a low growl. She clutched it, praying he hadn't heard. Trying not to think of food, she paused in front of her office and threw open the door.

Hamilton stood back, waiting for her to enter. She hesitated, wondering if she should sit behind her desk or allow him to do so. Deciding that it was her desk, and therefore her privilege, she marched past him and sat down. He took the chair opposite her, his expression set and unreadable.

When he didn't speak, she cleared her throat. "Perhaps you should start at the beginning."

Stretching out his legs, he contemplated his boots. "I came by earlier to discuss a matter with you that I thought might be of mutual interest. I intended to join you for supper, and when I saw no one in the corridors I realized I was a little late and I made directly for the dining room."

Still trying to get her thoughts around the matter of mutual interest that he'd mentioned, Meredith began, "I'm sorry I wasn't—"

"I reached the door," Hamilton rudely interrupted, "at the same time as Pratt. I—"

"Platt."

He glared at her. "Pardon me?"

"His name is Platt, as you know perfectly well. Why do you insist on calling him Pratt?"

"Pratt, Platt, what difference does it make? We are not here to discuss your unruly assistant. We are here to find out why you and your fellow tutors left the premises with only a neophyte tutor in charge, who obviously has no ability to control a group of rowdy students, allowing what could have been a small incident to get completely out of hand."

The hollow feeling in Meredith's stomach deepened. "Oh, dear heavens. What happened?"

"What happened, my dear Meredith, was that the entire student body of the Bellehaven Finishing School for Young Ladies erupted into a riot, such as I have not seen in my entire life.

"They were leaping about on the tables with food in their hair and all over their clothes, smashing dishes and generally behaving like guttersnipes instead of the elegant women we strive to produce in this honored establishment."

Struggling to breathe, Meredith murmured, "Oh, my. What did Mr. Platt have to do with all this?"

Hamilton looked taken aback. "What? Oh, nothing, as far as I know. Miss Montrose, however, stood in the middle of the room, wailing like a banshee instead of ordering an end to that disgusting display of atrocious manners."

Meredith wasn't sure if it was hunger, or her quivering nerves, or the fact that he had called her 'my dear Meredith,' albeit with a certain amount of sarcasm. Whatever it was, the urge to laugh became too strong to subdue.

It began as a whimper, then a giggle, then, in spite of her efforts to control it, the laughter spluttered out in a torrent of mirth.

For a moment Hamilton's face was scarlet with outrage, which only intensified Meredith's helpless hilarity. Then, as she fought for breath, the scowl slowly disappeared and the glimmer of a smile twitched at his lips.

"I fail to see what is so highly amusing," he said, though now his voice, contrary to his words, was tinged with humor.

"I'm sorry." Meredith gasped for breath and struggled for composure. "It was just . . . you're right, of course. The matter is quite serious. I shall be certain to call an emergency assembly tomorrow morning to address the situation. Rest assured, Mr. Hamilton—"

"Stuart."

"—Stuart," she amended, the name seeming to stick to her tongue, "rest assured that nothing like this will ever"—she gulped down a latent giggle—"happen again. Not while I'm in charge, anyway."

Hamilton sat back and laced his fingers across his chest. "Which brings me to the point. Might I enquire why it was necessary for two of your tutors to accompany you on whatever errand you were engaged in this afternoon, thus leaving Miss Montrose to manage on her own?"

Meredith took a deep breath. How she hated having to make up these pesky excuses. To tell him the truth, however, would jeopardize any chance of her solving the murder and ridding herself of a very unwelcome ghost. "It wasn't exactly an errand. More an invitation, if you will."

Stuart raised a sardonic eyebrow. "Indeed? One that none of you could refuse, I take it?"

"Precisely." She gave him her warmest smile. "A dear friend is in trouble, and needed our help." As close to the truth as she dare go, she decided.

For a long moment he stared at her beneath lowered brows, then slowly let out his breath. "Very well. I will accept that the situation was unavoidable. I trust that in the future, however, you will make certain Miss Montrose is not left in such a vulnerable position again."

That stung, for some reason. Sylvia Montrose had been Stuart's choice to fill the vacancy left by Kathleen Duncan, Meredith's closest friend and fellow tutor, who had died from a blow to the head some months earlier.

As with Roger Platt, Stuart had insisted that he select the person for the job, giving Meredith not one say in the matter. In both cases, Meredith had vigorously protested. Neither of Stuart's choices had seemed particularly qualified for the role, and in Sylvia's case Meredith had taken an instant dislike to the woman.

She had convinced herself that it was because of Sylvia's way of finding fault with everything and everyone, but deep down she had a suspicion it might have to do more with the fact that Sylvia was younger and prettier, and seemed to be a special pet of Stuart Hamilton's.

"I believe," she said, choosing her words carefully, "that Miss Montrose is quite capable of learning how to take charge in a volatile situation, just as the rest of us had to do. One never knows when one will be subjected to rebellious behavior at Bellehaven. It could happen anywhere— in the classroom, in the living quarters, or out on the tennis court—and one can't always rely on additional help."

"Nevertheless, considering there are four tutors in this establishment, it seems feasible to expect at least one other person able to lend a hand. After all, in such cases, surely two figures of authority would present a more forceful deterrent to unacceptable behavior?"

"That isn't always possible. When we are taking classes we can't be forever running back and forth at someone's beck and call. It is therefore imperative that one learn to assess an unfortunate situation and act on a viable decision instead of crying for help at the slightest sign of discord. Miss Montrose should be every bit as accountable as the rest of us, and I refuse to make an exception in her case."

As always, whenever she so much as hinted that he gave preferable treatment to Sylvia, Hamilton's eyebrows drew together. "All that comes with experience," he said shortly. "Miss Montrose hasn't been here long enough to gain that kind of authority."

Meredith thinned her lips. "I think she has been here quite long enough." The words were out before she had considered them. Dismayed at her rashness, she waited for Stuart's reply.

Instead of responding, however, he got to his feet and tugged down the hem of his coat. "I can see you are exhausted by your engagement this afternoon, whatever that was. I shall leave you now to recover." He spun around and strode to the door.

Just as she was beginning to breathe easier, he turned, one hand on the doorjamb. "Just as a warning," he said quietly. "I do not appreciate being opposed without just cause. Nor do I appreciate being left in the dark about certain activities of my headmistress. I shall let it go for now, but I think you should know that my tolerance is wearing thin. Good day to you, Meredith."

Before she could answer him, the door had closed behind him.

Only then did she realize that he had failed to mention the matter of interest that had brought him to the school that afternoon.

Uttering a guttural sound in her throat, she picked up a ledger and flung it at the door. The resulting thud helped calm her temper, and she rose to retrieve the fallen book.

As she did so, a familiar sight brought her to a halt. Staring into the corner of the room, she said loudly, "What do you want now?"

The pink mist swirled around itself, spinning gradually into a frothy cloud, until eventually the figure of James Stalham appeared in the middle.

It took Meredith a moment or two to realize that the mist had not turned red this time. Eying the apparition warily, she announced, "I have just visited the Stalham estate."

James nodded.

"I now believe that you did not kill your father."

For a moment the mist turned red at the edges, and she hurried to reassure him. "I am doing my best to find out what really happened that night." She hesitated, as he continued to stare at her, then added, "I think perhaps Pauline Suchier might have shot your father."

James violently shook his head.

Frustrated, she stared at him. "You disagree? How could you know for certain that Miss Suchier was not responsible for your father's death? You said yourself at the trial that she was the subject of an argument between you and Lord Stalham."

This time, while shaking his head again, James raised his hands and waved them as if dismissing someone.

Meredith narrowed her eyes. "Do you know something, perhaps, that didn't come out at the trial?"

This time she was rewarded with a nod. "So please, tell me what it is."

James began mouthing words, and she stopped him with a raised hand. "I can't read your lips." She sighed in frustration. "I don't know why I can't when I can read everyone else's, but I can't, so you will have to find another way to tell me what you know."

James responded by flattening his palm as if he were pressing against a wall.

Meredith frowned. "I don't understand. What are you doing? Opening a door?"

James shook his head, and pushed his palm farther away from him. When Meredith failed to react, he kept bringing up his hand and pushing it out until finally she cried out, "I don't understand what you are doing!"

At that moment a loud rapping on the door made her jump out of her skin. "Meredith?" It was Felicity's voice and she sounded concerned. "Are you all right?" The door opened, and her friend peered in. "What are you doing in here? Talking to yourself?"

Meredith glanced over at the corner, but as she'd expected, the mist had vanished. "Not exactly," she said carefully.

Felicity's expression changed. "You were talking to the ghost."

"Shhh!" Meredith put a finger against her lips. "Someone might hear you."

"There's nobody here to hear me." Felicity came all the way into the room. "What did the dratted thing do this time?"

Meredith sighed. "James didn't do anything. At least, he tried to tell me something, but I couldn't understand what it was."

Felicity made a face. "That's a shame. He could be telling you who killed his father, and you could be finished with all this sleuthing."

"Oh, if only that were so." Meredith's stomach growled again, reminding her that she hadn't eaten anything since midday. "I think we should go to the kitchen and find out what Mrs. Wilkins has left for us."

"Good idea. I'm so hungry I could eat a cow." Felicity held up her hand as Meredith started for the door. "But first, I'd like to know what Hamilton had to say. That's if you're at liberty to tell me."

Meredith didn't like the gleam in her friend's eyes. "Why wouldn't I be? Anything that Mr. Hamilton says to me I most certainly can pass along to you. I assume the students told you what happened in the dining room this evening?"

"I heard there was a food fight, and things got a little noisy. Until Hamilton arrived and ordered everyone to their rooms."

"Yes, well, that's what he told me." Meredith walked to the door. "He was also extremely displeased that the three of us had left Sylvia Montrose alone to handle things. He said she wasn't prepared for such an awesome responsibility."

She hadn't been able to keep the resentment out of her voice and Felicity grunted in disgust. "Is that man so obtuse he can't see past his nose? If you ask me, he knows he made a mistake in hiring her, as well as that disgusting Roger Platt, and simply refuses to acknowledge his misjudgment. He really is quite insufferable. Then again, I haven't yet met a man who isn't intolerable."

Meredith was inclined to agree that there was some truth to Felicity's observations about Stuart's defense of his choices, but her complaining stomach wouldn't allow her to dwell on it now. "Where is Essie? She needs to put some food in her stomach, too, or she won't be able to sleep tonight."

Felicity stepped out into the hallway. "She went down to the kitchen while I came looking for you. She was faint from hunger and I thought it best to send her along."

"Very considerate of you." Meredith closed the door to her office. "Now let's join her, before we both collapse."

Chapter 13

"We have to call off the protest," Grace said, as she pulled a plate out of the steaming water in the kitchen sink and handed it to Olivia. "Now that all the students are in detention all weekend, they can't possibly go to the village. Everyone will be watching to make sure nobody leaves the rooms."

Olivia smacked the plate down on the draining board so hard Grace was sure it would break. "I'm not going to give up the plan. We have to think of a way to get them out of the school without anyone seeing them."

"How are you going to do that?"

"I don't know. But I'll think of something."

Grace frowned as she dug into the dishwater again. Swirling her fingers around to find the knives and forks, she wished with all her heart that Olivia would, at the very least, postpone the protest. She couldn't see what difference it made if they waited another week. Though come to think of it, without the May Day celebrations it would be a lot harder to escape the eagle eye of P.C. Shipham. The detestable village constable had a nasty habit of turning up at the worst possible moment.

She dragged a handful of cutlery out of the water and dropped it onto the draining board. Either way, she thought gloomily, they were heading for trouble and she was going to be right in the middle of it. As usual.

"I've got it!" Olivia shouted, making Grace jump so hard she dropped a saucer. It sunk back into the water, luckily without shattering.

"What exactly have you got?" Mrs. Wilkins asked from the doorway.

Grace uttered a squeak of dismay and Olivia shook her head at her. "I've got the plate she nearly dropped," she said, holding it up. "Look, it's all in one piece."

The cook advanced into the kitchen, a frown creasing her face. "Just as well," she muttered, as she headed for the pantry. "What with all the plates that got smashed, we'll be lucky to have enough for breakfast tomorrow. I can't imagine what got into those girls tonight. Something must have set them off."

Grace and Olivia exchanged glances. Just before Stuart Hamilton had roared his commands, Grace had heard the girls chanting. There was not a single doubt in her mind that the brawl had started because of the proposed protest. Whenever the subject of women's rights came up, emotions tended to get stirred up. Some of the students thought that the suffragettes were disgracing the image of women, and were violently opposed to the protests. Invariably that caused some fierce arguments on both sides.

Grace stared at her friend and mouthed, "Now what?"

Olivia raised a closed fist in the air. "We still go," she mouthed back.

Mrs. Wilkins emerged from the pantry carrying a tray of sandwiches. "You two, get back up to the dining room and clean up that mess up there. It all has to be spick-and-span before any of us get to bed tonight."

"What about the washing up?" Grace asked, pointing a finger at the stack of dirty dishes.

"Put them all in the sink to soak." The cook laid the tray on the table. "By the time you get back they'll be clean and you can leave them to drain on the draining board. You can put them away in the morning."

Grace wiped her hands on her apron, while Olivia threw down her tea towel.

"First thing in the morning, mind," the cook called after them as they rushed for the door. "And take oil lamps with you. All the gas lamps have been turned off in there."

"Yes, Mrs. Wilkins!" they chorused together, then fled for the dining room.

Arriving breathless at the door, Grace pushed it open. Holding up her lamp, she walked inside and up to the first table. The chaos that met her eyes made her gasp. The remains of food lay everywhere, splattered all over the benches and the floor—even on the walls. Broken dishes lay scattered about and someone had taken off her shirt-waist and thrown it up over a rung of the gas chandelier.

Grace's eyes widened. "Look at that. It's a wonder it didn't catch fire and burn the place down."

Olivia set her lamp down on the end of the table, making it even easier to see the mess created by the rebelling students. "I know. I saw it when we were in here before. That's what gave me the idea."

Grace frowned at her. "What idea?"

"The idea of how we can get the girls out of here without being noticed."

"And how, exactly, are we going to do that?"

"It's easy." Olivia grinned, her teeth reflecting white in the flickering light from her lamp. "We start a fire. While everyone is in here trying to put it out, we smuggle our protestors out the back door."

Speechless, Grace could only stand staring at her with her mouth open. She must not have heard right. Surely, *surely,* Olivia wasn't planning on burning down the school just to hold a protest?

"This is so kind of you, Mrs. Wilkins." Meredith helped herself to another sandwich and glanced at Felicity and Essie, both of whom were munching away as if it were to be their last meal.

"Not at all, Mrs. Lewellyn. Happy to do it, I'm sure." If the cook was curious as to why all three tutors were in her kitchen late in the evening, eating sandwiches instead of a nice meal, she gave no indication. "If you'll excuse me, though, I think I'll toddle off to bed. I have to be up early in the morning."

Feeling a little guilty about keeping her working so late, Meredith waved her hand. "Oh, please, do go. We will tidy up here when we're finished."

"Oh, don't bother. The maids will see to it." The cook smiled. "It will keep them out of mischief. Those two can be quite a headache at times, that they can."

"It does seem, though, that Olivia and Grace have been behaving themselves quite well lately." Meredith placed the thick, roast pork sandwich on her plate. "I hope they learned their lesson from the last time they were in trouble."

"Oh, I certainly hope so, m'm." Mrs. Wilkins placed

a hand over her heart and walked back to the table, making Meredith wish she had ended the conversation, leaving her free to eat her sandwich. "But I can't help feeling they're up to something again. They've had their heads together quite a few times lately, and then they shut up whenever I get near them. That's not a good sign."

Meredith felt a pang of uneasiness. "No, it isn't. I've noticed the students are a little restless, too, but I put it down to the approach of summer. This time of year always seems to stir their blood, for some reason."

"Yes, m'm. Well, I just hope that's all it is this time. I gave both the maids a good talking to, I did, and I hope they took it to heart. They are so caught up in this women's rights movement these days. All this nonsense is going to get them put in jail, I told them. Then where would they be? Mr. Hamilton would never let them come back here once they got out, that's for certain."

At the mention of Hamilton's name, Meredith paled. "Well, keep a stern eye on them, Mrs. Wilkins. Let us hope this is no more than a case of spring fever."

"Amen." Mrs. Wilkins crossed herself and left.

"What was all that about?" Felicity reached for a bacon sandwich.

"I don't know," Meredith said slowly, "but I have a rather nasty feeling that something is brewing in the wind. We had better stay on our toes, ladies, or we might once again have cause to bring the wrath of Mr. Hamilton down on our heads."

Having slept through the night without any interruptions from the ghost of James Stalham, Meredith arose the next morning feeling a little more optimistic. The sun was shining, the birds sang in the trees outside her window, and today was the first of May. Summer, with all its glorious warm sunshine, the tennis and croquet tournaments, perhaps an afternoon or two punting on the river and walks among the fragrant blossoms in the gardens, was only a few weeks away.

Throwing open her window, Meredith pulled in a deep, deep breath of cool, fresh air. It smelled of newly cut grass and the fragrance of lilac. It was Saturday. Time for a nice walk in the grounds to see what Tom, the gardener, had been planting lately.

She turned back to the room, her gasp rising in her throat when she saw the pink mist swirling in the corner. "Oh, no. Not you again."

James seemed agitated, and kept disappearing, only to appear for a brief moment before vanishing again in the folds of the pink cloud.

Alarmed, Meredith edged closer to him. "Wait, don't go."

Her powers had an unfortunate way of weakening just at the crucial time when she needed the contact the most.

Staring at the thinning mist, she held out her hand. "Be strong, James. I know I haven't made much progress, but I'll keep trying. I'll go back there and talk to Smithers."

At her mention of the butler, the mist grew dense and dark. Angry red coils of vapor spiraled around the image of the aristocrat. His eyes burned with hostility, and his lip curled, baring his teeth and frightening Meredith out of her wits.

"I take it you don't like Smithers," she said, shrinking back when James raised his fist and punched the air. "Well, I don't like him, either. Is there any specific reason you hate him so?"

James grabbed his throat, tilted his head on one side, and stuck out his tongue.

Immediately Meredith felt remorse. "Oh, of course. It was because of his testimony that you were convicted."

James straightened his head, his eyes flashing in agreement.

He mouthed something and she shook her head.

"I'm sorry, I—"

She broke off as James cupped a hand over his mouth, then flapped his fingers against his thumb and violently shook his head.

"You're saying he lied!" she said, with a rush of triumph. "I know. He lied about someone else being there that night. Pauline Suchier was there."

James nodded, then began to fade rapidly into the swirling folds of the mist.

"And your mother," Meredith added.

For a brief moment James's face registered shock and disbelief, and then he was gone, the remnants of the mist curling down to the floor before disappearing altogether.

He hadn't known. Meredith walked over to her bed and sat down. If Lady Clara had been at the house that night, James had no knowledge of it. Why hadn't his mother spoken up when Smithers lied on the stand? Did she really believe her son was guilty of murder? Or had Winnie been mistaken about who she'd seen that night?

She should talk to Lady Clara, Meredith thought, as she climbed to her feet. But that meant a trip to London, and that wouldn't be possible until half term, which was still six weeks away.

She would go back to the estate instead, alone this

time, and confront Smithers with what she knew. It might also help if she had a word with Inspector Dawson. He might be able to give her some advice. He was far more approachable than P.C. Shipham and, being his superior, in a better position to advise her.

Besides, she rather enjoyed talking to the enigmatic policeman, and it was May Day, after all. The students were all confined to their rooms for the day. She had plenty of time to do whatever she wanted, and perhaps even enjoy some of the festivities in the village before she had to return.

When she announced her plans to Felicity and Essie in the teacher's lounge later, they both seemed put out to be excluded. "I don't like the idea of you going back to that place alone," Felicity said, while Essie sat biting her fingernails. "I don't trust that butler. He has an evil look in his eyes."

"I'm sure he's quite harmless," Meredith murmured, being sure of no such thing. "He's more likely to talk to me if I'm on my own."

"If he didn't tell Essie much of anything, what gives you the idea he'll talk to you?"

Essie looked alarmed. "I don't want to go back there. That man frightens me."

"He's told Essie all he's going to tell her." Meredith buttoned up her coat and picked up her gloves. "I need to confront him myself and try to get the truth out of him. So far, all we have is suspects."

"At least two," Felicity muttered. "Pauline Suchier for one, and possibly Lady Clara, though I have to agree with Essie that she's an unlikely candidate, mostly because it's hard to imagine a mother allowing her son to hang for a crime she committed."

"Anything is possible. It seems quite a few people lied about what was going on that night."

"Either lied or left out important evidence." Meredith pulled on the other glove. "In any case, since Smithers was the first one to arrive on the scene, I might learn something that could help us sort all this out."

"Well, at the very least," Felicity said, looking far from reassured, "since the students are all confined to their rooms and we're not all needed here, why don't you meet us later this afternoon on the village green. We can all enjoy the dancing together."

Meredith smiled. "That sounds like a marvelous idea. Shall we say about two o'clock? I believe the dancing begins at that time."

"Two o'clock it is."

As Meredith turned to leave, Felicity added urgently, "Be careful, Meredith. Don't take any undue chances."

"I'll be careful." Meredith paused at the door. "I shan't be quite alone, you know. I shall have Reggie with me, if the need for help should arise."

Felicity frowned. "Is that supposed to make us feel better?"

Essie uttered a nervous giggle. "Any port in a storm."

"Exactly." With a casual wave of her hand, Meredith sailed out the door.

Mrs. Wilkins glanced up at the clock, gritting her teeth in frustration. She'd sent the maids to fetch the dirty dishes at least an hour ago. Where the devil were they? They should have been back long before this.

With an annoyed clicking of her tongue, the cook pulled off her apron. She would have to go and look for the pesky girls. It was bad enough that they'd had to serve breakfast in the rooms this morning, thanks to Mr. Hamilton's orders. Not that the students would take too much notice of that. They were very good at coming up with excuses why they weren't in their rooms for inspection.

The problem was, it had taken much longer than usual to serve up all those breakfast trays, disrupting her schedule, and now she had to wait for the maids to bring back all those trays, get the dishes washed and dried and then get ready for the midday meal, which was going to be really late at this rate. Drat Stuart Hamilton. What the heck did he know about school schedules anyway?

Muttering and moaning to herself, she headed for the door. Just as she reached it, the most dreadful clanging echoed down the hallway outside. Enough to give her a headache. Unbelievable. Why in heaven did the teachers decide to hold a fire drill today of all days? Didn't they know that the pupils were supposed to stay in their rooms?

Stomping up the kitchen steps, Mrs. Wilkins puffed and grunted, ready to let fly at the first person who had the misfortune to cross her path.

She reached the top of the steps, to be greeted by what sounded like a flock of agitated geese. Students streamed across the lobby, laughing and shoving each other in complete disregard for the rules of etiquette. Some were actually fighting to get through the door and out into the sunshine.

Mrs. Wilkins shook her head in disgust. The tutors would have their hands full this morning, all right. She searched the crowd of jostling students and caught sight of Miss Cross's head above the rest. The maids had to be on their way out, too. She wondered if they'd taken the trays down to the kitchen before joining everyone outside.

She was about to raise a hand to catch Miss Cross's attention when something else distracted her. Smoke. She could swear she could smell smoke.

For a moment she wondered if it was her imagination, triggered perhaps by the fire drill. Then she saw it—a wisp of smoke curling down the hallway that led to the dining room. Waiting no longer, she barged through the mass of giggling girls and shot out the door into the fresh air.

Chapter 14

In the upstairs hallway, Grace stood guard while Olivia herded about a dozen would-be protestors out of their rooms and down toward the stairs.

The main group of students had already left, and to Grace's relief, the stairwell remained empty as Olivia's troops headed her way. "You're quite sure the dining room won't catch on fire?" she muttered, as Olivia reached her. "It smells awfully smoky."

"I'm sure. The fire is probably out by now. I made sure the waist was tucked out of the way of the lamps." Olivia grabbed her arm and gave her a little push. "Come on, we have to get a move on. It's going to take us at least an hour to walk into the village and we have to be there before they start the maypole dancing."

"All right." Reluctantly, Grace started down the stairs. She had to be bonkers to be doing this, she told herself as the girls clambered down after her. They were bound to get caught, no matter what Olivia said.

Reaching the bottom, she held up her hand. The girls halted, all whispering among themselves until Olivia hissed at them to shut up.

Grace could hear the commotion in the lobby. They were still evacuating the premises. She looked back at Olivia. "Shouldn't we wait until they are all outside?"

Olivia shook her head. "There isn't time. It took longer than I thought it would for someone to ring the fire bell. We should have done it ourselves instead of waiting for someone else to notice the fire."

"You said it would look suspicious if we did it," Grace reminded her.

Sophie Westchester, at her usual position at the head of the crowd, raised her voice. "Are you going to stand there arguing all day or are we going to leave? For pity's sake, let's get on with it!"

A faint chorus of agreement answered her and Olivia shot up her hand. "Be quiet, you silly twerps. Someone will hear us and come back to get us. Then we won't be able to leave here at all."

"Here! Who are you calling a silly twerp?"

"Yeah," someone else called out. "You've got no right calling us silly twerps."

Olivia rolled her eyes. "All right, all right, let's get moving. Just follow me, all of you, and flipping well keep your mouths shut."

Grace stood aside and let Olivia squeeze past her, then followed her down the hallway to the back stairs. Shuffling feet behind her assured her the troops were following, and moments later they were all outside the building, huddled against the wall.

"How are we going to get down the driveway without

anyone seeing us?" Sophie demanded. "Do you plan to make us all invisible or something?"

Olivia gave her a scathing glance. "We're not going down the driveway, are we. We're going behind the tennis courts to climb over the back wall."

Shrieks and moans followed this announcement, and once again Olivia had to hold up her hand. "One more squeak out of any of you and you can stay here with the rest of the bloomin' bunch. If you want to come with us you'll have to be *quiet*!"

Sophie tilted her nose in the air. "All right, there's no need to get testy." She beckoned to her friends. "Come on, we can do this. It'll be a lot more fun than being cooped up in our rooms for the rest of the day."

Muttering in agreement, the girls lined up behind her. Sophie glared at Olivia. "All right, Sergeant Major. Lead the way."

With a nod of approval, Olivia crept forward to the corner of the building. "Everyone's out there in the court-yard," she muttered, when she came back. "They won't see us if we crouch over and hurry across the lawns to the tennis courts. We'll all wait there for everyone to catch up and then we'll climb over the wall. There's a really big tree there to help us climb up and over."

Grace sent a silent prayer skyward as she rushed across the lawn, bent nearly double in compliance with Olivia's instructions, and expecting hoarse shouts to erupt any minute ordering them back to the courtyard.

She could hear faint giggles behind her, and lots of shushing, until they finally reached the tennis courts, all slightly out of breath. Crowding behind the fence, they waited for Olivia's next orders.

Her face flushed with importance and exertion, Olivia waved her arm at the oak tree growing on the other side of the wall. "See that branch," she said, her voice still low in spite of the fact that no one could possibly hear her with all the noise they were making in the courtyard. "That's what we have to climb on to get over the wall."

Grace stared at it in alarm. The lowest branches looked really high off the ground. Before she could say anything, however, Olivia was charging across the grass toward the wall, and all she could do was follow her, and pray that no one broke a leg or something worse.

Meredith peered out the window as Reggie halted the carriage in front of the Stalham mansion. She had caught sight of someone walking through the gardens as they had traveled up the driveway, and suspected it might be Winnie.

Sure enough, the maid turned the corner just as Meredith climbed out of the carriage. For a moment Winnie hesitated, then turned around and disappeared again.

"I think I'll go in the back entrance," Meredith announced, as Reggie closed the door with a loud thud.

He looked at her in surprise. "Pardon me, m'm, but isn't that a little unusual?"

"Perhaps, but I have my reasons."

Reggie's expression changed. "Pardon me for asking, m'm, and correct me if I'm wrong, but you are after a murderer, aren't you?"

Meredith avoided looking at him. "Perhaps."

"Then I don't think you should go in there alone, m'm. Remember the last time you took it upon yourself to go after a killer? You almost ended up getting killed yourself. I think, since you're going in the back entrance, that I should come with you."

"It will be more difficult to find out what I need to know if I have someone with me." Meredith gave him a reassuring smile. "Besides, it would be even more difficult to explain your presence. Just wait for me here, and if I haven't returned after a reasonable amount of time, then you have my permission to come and look for me."

Reggie swiped a lock of his fair hair away from his eyes.

"Well, if you say so, m'm, but if anything happened to you, I'll never forgive meself. So help me, I won't."

Meredith touched his arm. "Thank you, Reggie. I deeply appreciate your concern. Rest assured I shall take pains to return unscathed. Now make yourself comfortable and I shall be as quick as I can be. We have to be at the police station in Witcheston and back again before two o'clock this afternoon. I'm supposed to be meeting Miss Cross and Miss Pickard at the village green. We plan to watch the dancing."

Reggie's eyes lit up. "The maypole dancing. That's good. I'd like to see that meself."

"Good. Then we have something to look forward to, don't we."

Leaving him, she hurried around the corner and made her way across the yard to the tradesmen's entrance. To her relief, Winnie answered the door to her knock.

The maid's eyes widened, and she looked nervously over her shoulder before exclaiming, "Mrs. Llewellyn! Whatever are you doing at this door?"

"I came to have a word with you." Without being asked, Meredith stepped through the door and into the kitchen.

Mrs. Parker stood at the stove, busily stirring something in a large pot that smelled wonderful.

Meredith made a mental note to have a bite to eat once she arrived in Witcheston. No doubt Reggie would be happy, too, with a sandwich from his favorite pub.

"It's Mrs. Llewellyn," Winnie announced, as the housekeeper glanced over her shoulder.

Mrs. Parker uttered an exclamation and spun around to stare at Meredith. "Mrs. Llewellyn! Whatever are you doing in the kitchen?"

"I came to have a quick word with Winnie," Meredith explained. "I shan't keep her long."

The housekeeper frowned. "What do you want to talk to her about, if I may ask?"

"Just a few questions about her work in the house. I'll need to know if I'm to hire a new maid."

"Well, pardon me, m'm, but why on earth didn't you use the front entrance?"

Meredith smiled. "To be perfectly honest, I was hoping to avoid Smithers. I find him rather intimidating."

"He'll be even more nasty if he sees you in here." She sent a nervous glance over her shoulder. "I hope you're not here to ask more questions about the murder. Mr. Smithers said if you came back asking questions I was to go straight to him so he could throw you out."

Meredith decided that the time for pretense was over. "Mrs. Parker, I'm sorry I misled you in the beginning, but the truth is, I am acquainted with a very close friend of James Stalham. He has sent me to find out what I can about the night his father died. He is convinced, as I know both of you must be, that James did not kill his father. I'm trying to find out who did, so I can clear James Stalham's name."

For a long moment the housekeeper stared at her, her

eyes wide with shock and fear. "We don't know nothing other than what we told you. Besides, anything you want to ask Winnie, you can ask her right here in front of me."

Meredith thought fast. "The longer I'm in the kitchen, Mrs. Parker, the more chance there is that Smithers will come in and find me. However, if you want to take that chance, it's entirely up to you."

"Can't you just leave? I told you we don't know anything else."

Meredith walked over to the table and sat down. "Nevertheless, I'd like to ask Winnie a few more questions. I don't intend to leave until I have done so."

Mrs. Parker aimed a desperate look at the clock on the wall, then nodded at Winnie. "Take Mrs. Llewellyn to my room. She can talk to you there. And be quick about it. I need you to peel some potatoes for me."

"Yes, Mrs. Parker."

"There's just one question I'd like to ask you before I go." Meredith got up and moved toward the door. "Why didn't you mention that the stable boy, Edward, is your son?"

The housekeeper's face turned red, and she dropped her gaze. "I didn't want you to go thinking he'd come back to seek revenge on the master." She looked up again. "He'd never do such a thing. I swear it!"

Meredith nodded. "I'm sure you're right." Leaving the distraught woman watching after her, she followed Winnie out the door.

Winnie's face seemed pinched with anxiety as she led the way down the hallway. Once inside the cozy room, she stood by the door, her fingers twisting in her apron while Meredith seated herself on one of the comfortable chairs.

"Winnie," she began, "I'd like to know exactly what you saw and heard the night Lord Stalham was shot."

Winnie looked as if she was about to be sick. "I told you everything I know, m'm. I didn't see nothing until the constables got here and after a while I saw them taking away Mr. James."

"Mrs. Parker said she saw you in the hallway when she came down the stairs that night. So you must have arrived there before she did."

"Oh, yes, m'm. I did." Winnie sent a hunted look at the door, as if she was about to dash through it.

"That was after you thought you saw Lady Clara on the back stairs, I presume?"

"Yes, m'm. It were." Winnie nodded so hard her cap slipped over her eyes. Pushing it back, she added, "It was right after that."

"I see." Meredith kept her gaze on the maid's face. "But you didn't tell anyone that you thought you saw Lady Clara that night."

"No, m'm, I didn't." Winnie shifted from one foot to the other. "I didn't want to get her into trouble, that's what. I didn't want to be the one what got her taken away for shooting her husband."

Meredith raised her eyebrows. "Are you saying you think Lady Clara shot Lord Stalham?"

"Oh, no, m'm, I'm not saying that at all." Winnie edged closer to the door. "I'm just saying that Lady Clara was always angry at Lord Stalham. Always shouting at him, she was. I was afraid if I'd told on her the constables might have thought she'd done it."

Meredith stood and walked toward the maid, her gaze fixed firmly on Winnie's face. "Do you have any idea at all who shot Lord Stalham, Winnie?"

The maid backed away, one hand reaching for the door handle. "No, m'm, I don't. But whoever it was, he did us all a favor. Lord Stalham was a horrible man. Horrible." Bursting into tears, she pulled the door open and rushed outside.

Meredith heard her footsteps pounding down the hallway, then all was silent. Shaking her head, she headed for the door. Outside in the hallway she paused, her mind occupied with her conversation with Winnie. She had the feeling again that she was missing something important. Something that Winnie had said. If only she could remember. . . .

"Mrs. Lewellyn!"

She jerked up her head at the sound of the harsh voice. She hadn't heard the footsteps come up behind her, yet there he was, as dark and menacing as ever, his face a mask of disdain. "Why, Smithers, you gave me quite a start." She smiled at him, and received a cold stare for her trouble.

"Mrs. Llewellyn, I don't know why you persist in intruding on us, but I think you should know that I'm aware that your interest in purchasing this property is pure fabrication. You are, in fact, a tutor, employed at the Bellehaven Finishing School, and you most certainly do not have the means to purchase this estate. I can't imagine why you are indulging in this masquerade, but I suggest you leave now."

She nodded. "Have no fear, I am leaving. In fact, I was just on my way out."

This seemed to have little effect on his irritation. "Just in case you are tempted to return, madam, I should warn you that should you attempt to do so, I shall have you prosecuted for trespassing."

Meredith thinned her lips. "I don't like threats, Mr. Smithers. Particularly from a servant."

His eyes darkened with indignation. "I might be a servant, madam, as you so ungraciously put it, but I am in charge of this residence and have the authority to throw you out if such a need should arrive."

Meredith raised her chin. "There is no need to be uncivil. As I said, I was on the point of leaving when you rudely accosted me. However, there is a question I should like answered before I leave, and I believe it's in your best interest to give me a satisfactory answer."

Wariness flickered across his face, and he took his time answering her. "And that is?"

"I should like to know why you lied on the stand when giving evidence at James Stalham's trial. That could cause you a great deal of trouble if revealed to the proper authorities. Perjury, I believe they call it."

Smithers wasn't quite able to hide his discomfort. "I have no idea what you mean."

"Oh, I think you do." Meredith crossed her arms to hide the fact that her hands shook. "You testified that no one else was in the house the night of the murder, yet I believe you were fully aware that at least one person had visited that evening. Maybe two."

"I beg your pardon?"

"Miss Pauline Suchier and Lady Clara were both at the house that night."

As she'd hoped, the butler instantly reacted. "That is simply not so!" It was the most animated she had ever seen him. A spot of red appeared in each cheek and he jerked his hands in protest. "I did not lie. What I said was that no one else was in the house at the *time* of the murder. I admit that Miss Suchier might possibly have paid Lord

Stalham a visit earlier. Since however, she had left before the murder took place, I saw no need to implicate her in the matter, thus causing unnecessary distress for . . . the family."

"For Lady Clara, you mean. She was here that night, wasn't she?"

The butler's face was once more a mask. "Not to my knowledge, no."

Meredith nodded. "It's as I thought. You're protecting her."

Smithers raised his chin. "May I remind you again, Mrs. Llewellyn, that you are trespassing on private property. Please leave at once and do not return, or I will be forced to take some most unpleasant measures."

Jolted by the venom in his eyes, Meredith took a step back. "You have no need to be concerned. I have no wish to return, thank you." Lifting the hem of her skirt, she swept down the hallway to the front door.

Once outside, she could breathe easier again. Her encounter with Smithers had unnerved her, and she was still shaking when she reached the carriage. She had hoped to learn something useful that she could take to Inspector Dawson, other than her somewhat neophyte instincts, but having drawn a blank in that regard, she would have to rely on the inspector's experience and powers of deduction.

Reggie seemed relieved to see her, and wasted no time in urging Spirit into a fast trot. Since she had suggested stopping by the Pig and Whistle on the way for a sandwich and a glass of cider, she felt quite sure they would arrive in Witcheston in record time.

Chapter 15

"How much farther is it?" Sophie Westchester wiped a band of perspiration from her forehead with her sleeve. "I don't think I can walk another step."

A chorus of petulant voices rose in agreement. Olivia halted so suddenly the students behind her started bumping into one another.

Grace, who had been forced to a halt behind her friend, received a hefty shove in the back that sent her forward into Olivia.

"Ouch!" Grace turned around to glare at Sophie, who was directly behind her. "What'd you do that for?"

"I didn't do it." Sophie jerked a thumb over her shoulder. "She bumped into me."

"I couldn't help it. Maria bumped into me!" said the girl behind her.

This was repeated all the way back until Olivia held up her hand. "For gawd's sake shut *up*! The lot of you! What a bunch of sickly babies you are. You're supposed to be suffragettes, strong and brave, ready to defend rights for women against all odds. You—"

"Oh, put a sock in it," Sophie said rudely. "We all know what a suffragette is—someone who thinks she can change the world by acting like a common hoodlum. Going around breaking things and smashing windows. What good is that going to do? Men are never going to treat us any better, or give us the vote, no matter what we do, so why bother?"

Grace held her breath as Olivia's face turned red. If there was one thing she'd learned, it was that Olivia flew into a rage at the mere hint that her beloved suffragettes were wasting their time.

Olivia advanced on Sophie, eyes flashing fire. "The protests *will* get us the vote," she said, her voice deceptively quiet. "As well as a lot of other things that women can't get just because they *are* women. People like Emmaline and Christabel Pankhurst, who sacrifice everything to raise protests against the government, won't stop fighting until they make the world a better place for all of you and all of your female children. Maybe not tomorrow, or next year, but one day, and when that happens, women all over the world will go down on their knees and thank us. So, if you don't want to be treated like a human being instead of an object put on this earth to serve men, then you don't belong here with us. Go back to school and your dopey little Roger Platt and see where that gets you."

Gasps from the other students greeted this outburst, while Sophie stood like a stone, her face rigid with shock. "How dare you speak to me like that, you . . . you . . . underling!"

Olivia looked about to retaliate, and Grace hurried to intervene. "If we are going to reach the pub before it closes we should be getting along." She tugged on Olivia's arm. "We need to hurry, Olivia, or your protest will never take place."

Scowling, Olivia nodded. "All right. Now listen to me, all of you. I have explained why we are doing this. If any of you don't feel strongly enough about it to do what we have to do, then you'd better go back now."

"We're here to get out of being stuck in our rooms," someone said. Others murmured in agreement.

Olivia exchanged an exasperated glance with Grace. "No, ladies, we are not here for the fun of it. Once we get to the village you will have to do exactly as I do. That means smashing every glass you can reach in the pub. Are you all with me?"

A few doubtful murmurs of assent answered her.

Olivia raised her voice. "We are going to show those chauvinistic pigs that we are worth something, that we are just as capable as any man, and that if we put our minds to it, we can rule the world. We refuse to be downtrodden slaves to men anymore. Now—*are you with me*?"

This time a satisfactory number of voices shouted a fervent response.

Triumphant, Olivia looked at Sophie. "Well?"

Sophie shrugged. "I suppose I might as well come along."

"Good. Then no more whining. Ladies, *march*!"

Falling in step behind her, Grace stared at Olivia's back in admiration. If only she could be like her, she thought, as they started down the hill on the final stretch to the village. Olivia was so strong, so confident, so certain that what she was doing was right and just, and that she would be rewarded for her efforts.

Grace wished fervently that she could believe that.

She'd lived long enough to know, however, that people like her and Olivia never got what they felt they deserved. You had to be born into a rich family to have a good life, with nice clothes and a lovely home and money to spend.

Otherwise all you had to look forward to was working your fingers to the bone looking after someone else's house, unless some poor sod came along and married you and then you spent the rest of your life working your fingers to the bone to take care of him and the children.

Still, she had to admit, it would be rather nice to be able to strike back once in a while. Just as long as they didn't get caught, that was. It might actually be rather satisfying to smash all those beer glasses in a place where women were deemed not fit to enter.

Hanging onto that thought, she marched down the main street of the village, chanting to herself, "Votes for Women. Equal rights for all!"

The street, usually crowded with Saturday shoppers, seemed unusually quiet. A few tired-looking women lined up in the doorway of the butcher's shop, and two more ladies struggled out of the greengrocer's hauling bulging shopping bags.

Having reached the door of the pub, Olivia halted and held up her hand. Nodding at the church clock across the street, she announced, "The maypole dancing should begin in about half an hour. Everyone will be on the village green by now, so we shouldn't have any trouble. When we go in, run through the public bar and grab all the glasses you can find and chuck them on the floor."

"It doesn't sound very quiet in there," one of the students said, as loud laughter erupted from inside the pub.

Noticing Olivia's anxious expression, Grace began to worry.

Just a few old men, Olivia had said. Too old and feeble to stop them. That laughter didn't sound as if it was coming from old men. In fact, it sounded a lot like—"

Her thoughts were interrupted when the door to the pub flew open. Billowing smoke drifted out, bringing with it the smell of cigars and beer. Two young men appeared in the doorway, and behind them the sound of vigorous male voices rose in a lusty cheer.

"Well, well," Sophie murmured, "this is looking a little more festive than I expected."

The two men in the doorway looked her over, in a way that made Grace even more nervous. "Hello, hello," one of them said. "What do we have here?"

Olivia, obviously realizing she was about to lose the element of surprise, leapt in front of the startled men. "Out of my way," she yelled, and gave one of them a hefty shove, sending him into his companion. "Come on, ladies, *charge!*" Before the men could recover, she had barged past them into the pub.

Sophie grinned at the men, then beckoned with her arm. "Come on, girls. This looks like fun."

With their boisterous cheers ringing in her ears, Grace waited for the excited students to enter the pub, then plunged through the door behind them and into the dark, smelly bar. For a moment she had trouble adjusting to the gloom, then she heard a loud crash and splintering of glass.

Turning toward the sound, she saw Olivia standing by a table full of young men, her arm raised and a glass of beer in her fist.

"Here, what the blue blazes are you doing?" One of

the young men leapt up to grab the glass, but Olivia was too quick for him. Down went the glass to shatter on the floor, spreading a pool of beer around it.

Three of the men jumped to their feet, holding their beer aloft so that Olivia couldn't reach it, while another grabbed her arms, holding her fast.

Grace charged forward to come to her aid, followed by the rest of the students. As they approached the table, several more men gathered around, until all the girls were surrounded.

Olivia struggled to get free, shouting, "Votes for women!" while Sophie swayed up to the closest male and fluttered her eyelashes. "I've never tasted beer," she said, gazing up at him with a puppy dog look on her face. "I've always wondered if I'd like it."

"Well, sweetheart, you can taste mine." The man had a soppy grin on his face as he tilted his glass for Sophie to sip the beer.

Grace expected Sophie to grab the glass and smash it on the floor, and judging by Olivia's expression, she expected the same thing. Instead, Sophie swallowed a mouthful of the beer amidst a roar of approval from the man's friends.

The man who'd been holding Olivia let go of her. Eyes blazing, Olivia appealed to the rest of the students. "Remember why we are here. Rights for women, remember?" She snatched a glass from another of the men and threw it down on the floor. Once more beer spread all around in a foaming mess.

"All right, that's enough." To Grace's dismay, two of the men grabbed Olivia and dragged her to the door.

Grace ran after them, pummeling on their backs. "Let her go, you brutes. How dare you!"

One of the men kicked the door open and pushed Olivia outside. Before Grace could protest again, rough hands propelled her out into the street. Stumbling up against the wall, she cracked her elbow, bringing tears to her eyes.

Olivia stood brushing her arms as if trying to get rid of the memory of those cruel hands.

Grace took a deep breath to steady her voice. "All right, now what?"

"Now," Olivia said, with a murderous gleam in her eyes, "we go back in and finish the job."

From the open window above Olivia's head, the sounds of girlish laughter mingled with the raised voices of the men.

"I don't think they are going to listen to you," Grace said, already having made up her mind that wild horses wouldn't drag her back in there.

"I'll make them listen to me," Olivia said, reaching for the door.

"They're having too good a time." Grace gestured at the window, where the noise had grown even more raucous. "Let's go home. We can have a protest another time, when only the old men are in there."

"I don't know where all these cheeky louts came from," Olivia muttered, "but I know they're not from the village. They don't belong here, so we have more right to be here than they do."

"I don't think they're going to see it that way," Grace began, but Olivia had already shoved open the door and marched back into the pub.

Sending up another desperate prayer, Grace followed her inside. Pure bedlam greeted her as she stood in the doorway, trying to adjust once more to the gloom.

Men were pushing and shoving to get near the students,

who seemed to be having a marvelous time, drinking from the beer glasses, chattering, laughing, and generally behaving in a most unladylike manner.

It occurred to Grace that should Mrs. Llewellyn find out about this, she'd flip her wig. Obviously Olivia's plan to smash all the glasses had failed miserably, and the best thing they could do was get the students out of the pub before they got into real trouble.

As it was, Grace could see the bartender ordering the girls off the premises, which fell on deaf ears, thanks to the loud protests of the men.

The sound of smashing glass turned her head. Unable to get near the tables because of the crush of men, Olivia had begun seizing tankards from over the bar. With a howl of protest, the bartender lunged for her, knocking the tankard from her hand to the floor. One more glass shattered.

Now the bartender was hollering at everyone to get out, holding onto Olivia's arms so she couldn't reach for any more glasses. Grace started forward to help her, but just then a stern voice spoke from right behind her.

"'Allo, 'allo! What's going on here, then?"

Turning, Grace met the disbelieving gaze of P.C. Shipham.

It was all too much for her. Closing her eyes, she let darkness overtake her and fell to the floor.

Meredith alighted from the carriage outside the Witcheston police station with a certain amount of pleasurable anticipation, not entirely due to the glass of cider she'd enjoyed at the Pig and Whistle.

She treasured her rare encounters with the quiet-spoken

inspector. A refreshing change from her volatile and somewhat discomfiting sessions with Stuart Hamilton.

She could relax and enjoy the conversation when in the inspector's presence, and that pleased her greatly. The fact that she also harbored a maternal instinct when she was with him was something she was reluctant to acknowledge.

True, the man's gaunt frame suggested he wasn't consuming enough good meals, and his expression often suggested he was weighed down by problems, no doubt connected to his work. Meredith suspected he had no wife to take care of his needs, but so far had lacked the courage to ask, since it was none of her business, anyway.

In fact, she had no idea why she should worry about him so. She hardly knew him, yet somehow he aroused her protective nature, and she invariably felt the urge to invite him to Bellehaven for a good meal and a relaxing glass of brandy.

It was odd, since to her knowledge Stuart Hamilton had no wife either, yet she had not wasted one minute of concern about his welfare. Probably because he gave every indication of being thoroughly capable of taking care of himself.

Seeing the inspector's smile as she entered his office raised her spirits. He greeted her warmly, and guided her to a comfortable chair before returning to his desk.

"It is always such a pleasure to see you, Meredith." He leaned back and folded his hands across his chest. "To what do I owe this most welcome visit? Not bad news, I trust?"

"Not exactly, Inspector." She set her handbag down by her feet. "I actually came to ask for your advice."

"Ah."

His eyes were green today—something else about him that fascinated her. Sometimes his eyes appeared to be blue, sometimes green, and although she could see the warmth in them when he looked at her, she could also detect a tinge of sadness, as if he had suffered a great loss. Maybe that was why she felt so sympathetic toward him.

Aware that she had been staring at him for far too long, she lowered her gaze. "It's about the murder of Lord Stalham."

The silence that greeted her announcement brought up her head. She could see that she'd shocked him, and wished she'd phrased her revelation a little less bluntly.

"That case is closed." Dawson frowned. "Lord Stalham's son, James, was convicted and hanged for the crime."

"Yes, I read the account of the trial in the newspaper."

"And so?"

With his watchful gaze on her face, she began to feel a little uncomfortable. She hadn't thought through exactly what she would say to him. After all, she could hardly explain about James's ghost, and how she came to suspect he had been innocent of the crime. Now that the moment was here, she hardly knew how to begin.

Curiosity crept into Edward Dawson's eyes as he continued to watch her. "Do you have something new in the case? Is that what you want to tell me?"

She let out her breath on a sigh. "I know this is going to sound odd to you, but I have reason to believe that James Stalham might not have been responsible for his father's death. Which means the real killer is alive and well, and has escaped justice."

Dawson's eyebrows almost disappeared in his hairline. "You have evidence to that effect?"

"No, I'm afraid I don't." She leaned forward. "I have, however, talked to the servants at the estate, and I know that Smithers omitted certain evidence when he gave his testimony on the stand."

"And that is?"

"He failed to testify that someone else was in the house that night. Miss Pauline Suchier."

To her surprise, the inspector nodded. "Yes, we are aware of that. Miss Suchier came to me and confessed that she had been present at the house that evening. She also had proof that she left there again, at least an hour before Lord Stalham was shot.

"Rather than reveal a notorious scandal, which would have served no purpose, seeing that Lord Stalham was deceased, we allowed the evidence to be left out of Smithers's testimony."

"Oh." Deflated, Meredith sank back on her chair. It seemed her theory about Pauline being the killer was false. But she continued to wonder about Lady's Clara's possible role, though everyone seemed determined to protect Lady Clara. Who, she wondered, had cared enough about James to protect him? She thought about telling the inspector that Winnie had seen Lady Clara in the house that night.

But had she? Winnie could have lied about that, but then why would she? There would be no point, considering that the case was over and James had paid for the crime. Unless she, too, believed that James wasn't guilty.

So, if James was innocent, and Winnie was telling the truth, that would mean his mother might well have killed his father. Yet Meredith still couldn't bring herself to believe that Lady Clara could stand by and watch her son die for her. No, it simply didn't make sense.

Winnie had to be mistaken. Perhaps it was Pauline Suchier she saw that night. There it was again . . . something else Winnie had said. If only she could remember.

Chapter 16

Aware that Inspector Dawson had spoken to her, Meredith shook off her thoughts. "I'm sorry, Inspector, I didn't quite catch that."

Again he smiled. "You seem preoccupied, Meredith. Is something worrying you? Why are you really here?"

"I don't know." She raised her hands and let them drop again. "I feel as though a grave miscarriage of justice has occurred, but unfortunately I have nothing to base my opinion on except instincts, and I have to admit, those are not very reliable."

Dawson leaned forward, his eyes now grave. "Even if that were so, I would need concrete evidence to support the theory, without which it would be impossible to launch another investigation."

"I understand." She reached for her handbag and stood. "I'm so sorry to have wasted your time."

Dawson rose swiftly to his feet and hurried around his desk.

"My dear Meredith, I can assure you, my time with you is never wasted. In fact, why don't you stay a while longer and share a pot of tea with me."

Still troubled, she smiled up at him. "There's nothing I'd like better, Inspector—"

"Edward, please."

"Edward, then. I'm sorry, but I promised my tutors I would meet them in Crickling Green at two o'clock and it must be close to that now."

Dawson pulled a pocket watch from his vest pocket and peered at it. "You have fifteen minutes," he said, tucking the watch back in his pocket. "Perhaps next time you will be able to stay longer."

"I should like that." She headed for the door and waited for him to open it.

Instead, he paused with his hand on the doorknob. "One question, if I may?"

"Of course."

"What reason exactly do you have to question James Stalham's conviction?"

She hesitated. "I am acquainted with a close member of the family, who has serious doubts about what actually happened that night. Speaking with the servants, I found there to be some severely conflicting statements, which leads me to wonder just who is telling the truth, and who is hiding it."

He frowned, a flicker of doubt crossing his face. "If you should happen across something concrete that I could use to reopen the investigation, please don't hesitate to get in touch with me."

"Of course I shall."

He reached for her hand, and raised it to his lips. "Until we meet again, then, Meredith."

Even through the fabric of her gloves, his touch burned, long after she had left him and was on her way back to the village.

Back in her carriage, as the fields and hedges sped by, she chided herself for her immature response. She allowed herself to be far too affected by the casual attentions of a man. Both Edward and Stuart seemed able to throw her into confusion with just a few words, a penetrating glance, and the touch of their lips on her hand.

They were two very different men, both with the ability to disturb her peace of mind. She had been too long without such consideration from the male species, she decided. Being completely surrounded by females day in and day out obviously took its toll.

Yes, she missed male companionship, but if she were completely honest, she would not trade her life for any other.

Not for all the Stuarts and Edwards in the world. She enjoyed her independence, such as it was, and the freedom to think, act, and accept anything she chose. It was a good life, rewarding and enjoyable, doing what she loved. There were not too many women who could claim as much.

Arriving at the village green, Reggie brought the carriage to a stop behind the bandstand. The chairs in front of the circular structure were filled with mostly ladies. A sea of wide-brimmed hats trimmed with feathers, flowers, and baubles almost hid their owners from view.

The orchestra, resplendent in their dark blue uniforms with gold epaulettes and gold-trimmed caps, played with rather more enthusiasm than skill, but the result was quite stirring, nevertheless.

Standing at the edge of the grass, Meredith scanned

the green for a glimpse of Felicity and Essie. The sun was warm enough to be felt through the cotton sleeves of her shirtwaist. Reggie had already taken the carriage to a more sheltered spot, where Spirit could enjoy a rest while his driver partook in the festivities.

Meredith made her way to the center of the green, where a crowd stood watching the dancers skip around the maypole skillfully weaving in and out with their colorful ribbons. Neither Felicity nor Essie seemed to be anywhere in sight, and Meredith began to wonder, since she had arrived a little late, if perhaps they had decided she wasn't going to join them after all and had wandered off elsewhere.

She was about to seek out Reggie and ask him to take her back to the school when she heard someone calling her name. Turning, she saw Essie hurrying across the grass, one hand holding onto her hat, the other clutching her skirt.

Red-faced with exertion, she reached Meredith and came to a stumbling halt. "The girls are in trouble," she said, panting for breath.

Concerned now, Meredith took hold of her arm and drew her into the shade of an ancient, twisted oak. "Take your time, Essie, and tell me what's happened."

"The girls!" Essie gulped and grasped Meredith's hand so tightly it hurt. "Oh, Meredith. The students. They've all been arrested!"

"I told you!" Grace sat shivering in the back room of the police station, her stomach knotted with anxiety. "I told you we'd get caught. What if we get the sack? What am I going to do without a job or somewhere to live? It's all right for you, Olivia, you have relatives you can go to, but I have nobody. I'll end up in the workhouse, I will."

Olivia rolled her eyes. "For pity's sake, Grace, stop your whining and let me think."

"Think? I think you've done enough thinking to last a lifetime. Why don't you listen to me? Why do you always have to go off and—"

Olivia leaned closer to Grace's ear. "Shut *up*! You're driving me bonkers. Wilky will get us out of this. She always does."

"Not this time. This time it isn't just us what got into trouble. It's a bunch of students as well. Mona won't stand for that. I tell you, Olivia. This is the end of it. We'll lose our jobs over this."

Olivia didn't even bother to answer her and Grace stared gloomily at the shiny black shoes poking out from under her skirt. She and Olivia had been separated from the students, and she could hear the girls arguing among themselves in the next room.

What if they all got expelled from the school? She and Olivia would be to blame. Everyone would hate them. Especially the teachers. That seemed even worse than being sacked, and tears began running down her cheeks at the thought.

She started as the door opened and a stern-faced P.C. Shipham looked in. "Come on, you two. I'm taking everyone back to Bellehaven."

Grace's stomach twisted even tighter. Now that it was time to face the music, she felt as if she would faint again. Oh, the disgrace. She'd never get another job. Unless she went to London. The thought of having to live in that big, bustling, dangerous city scared her to death. No, she couldn't do it. She'd die there, she just knew it.

"Come on." Olivia grabbed Grace's arm and dragged her off her chair. "We might as well go back and get it over with."

They passed through the main office of the police station, where an elderly man in shabby clothes leered at them as they walked close, his breath smelling worse than the public bar of the Dog and Duck.

Outside in the sunshine, as she breathed in fresh, clean-smelling air, Grace felt a little better. A black police wagon was lined up at the curb, pulled by a shiny black horse. P.C. Shipham had the back doors open and was pushing the students up and inside.

The girls didn't seem to mind. In fact, they were laughing and joking, their voices loud and their words slurred. Two or three of them were actually singing hymns, though horribly out of tune. Grace couldn't understand how they could be so happy when they were facing certain punishment.

Finally it was her turn to be helped into the wagon, though shoved was probably a better word. She landed on the floor, and Olivia tumbled in beside her. All the seats were occupied, so Grace made herself as comfortable as she could between the feet of the students seated on either side.

She had never been inside a police wagon before, though she'd once rescued Olivia from one in Witcheston. Staring at the bars on the window, Grace shivered. She felt like a criminal. What if they weren't taking her and Olivia back to school at all? What if they were going to take them to prison? Wasn't that what they did with the suffragettes when they caught them smashing things up?

It wasn't fair. She hadn't broken anything. It was Olivia what had broken the glasses, not her. Now she would have to pay for Olivia's sins, and that wasn't fair. Staring mournfully at her friend, she burst once more into tears.

Much to Meredith's relief, she arrived back at Bellehaven ahead of the police wagon. It had taken all her powers of diplomacy and persuasion to get the students and maids released. Not only that, she'd had to promise that there would be no more trouble from the students in the future—a promise almost impossible to keep.

All was quiet in the building when she walked in, followed by Essie. "I think I'd better talk to the students in the library," she said, as they stood in the quiet lobby. "Will you and Felicity wait here to make sure they are all present? I'll go to the library and wait there."

"Of course." Essie seemed close to tears. "I just can't believe they'd do such a thing," she added, her voice breaking. "After all we've taught them about the importance of etiquette and making a good impression. How could they sully their reputations that way? They were drinking ale, in a public bar, of all places, with all those unruly men. They were all *inebriated* for heaven's sake!"

Her voice had risen to a wail and Meredith shushed her. "Let's do our best to keep this quiet. If Mr. Hamilton ever got wind of this—"

"Speaking of Hamilton," Felicity said, from the open front door, "he's coming up the driveway right now."

Meredith gave her a stern glance. "That's not amusing, Felicity. This is no time for jocularity. The students have committed an unforgivable transgression and have threatened the reputation of this establishment. I—"

"I'm not joking, Meredith." Felicity pointed out the door. "Look for yourself."

Unable to believe her, Meredith hurried to the door and peered outside. Sure enough, Stuart Hamilton's carriage was bowling up the driveway and would arrive any second.

To make matters worse, turning in at the far end of the driveway was the black police wagon carrying two disobedient maids and thirteen drunken students.

"We have to shut him up somewhere," Meredith said, ice clutching at her stomach. "If he finds out what happened heaven knows what he'll do."

"Well, since you seem to have a way with him, you should be the one to keep him occupied," Felicity said, her smirk bringing heat to Meredith's cheeks. "Try to get him out of the way as soon as he walks in here and we'll get the students into the library."

"He's coming here to make sure we kept the students confined to their rooms," Meredith muttered. "For heaven's sake why can't he trust us?"

"I'd say the reason he can't is following him up the driveway this very minute," Felicity said dryly. "His timing is impeccable, as usual."

"Oh, for heaven's sake." Meredith stepped out onto the porch. "I'll try to attract his attention so that he doesn't turn around. Once I get him into my office, hustle the girls into the library and keep them there until I get rid of Stuart. I'll come to the library as soon as he's gone."

"Stuart?" Felicity's eyebrows shot up. "Since when have you been on a first name basis with Hamilton?"

Cursing herself for the slip, Meredith snapped, "Never mind that now. Just make sure you keep those students out of sight until after Mr. Hamilton has left."

"Oh, dear, oh, dear," Essie wailed. "What if he sees them? He'll know they've been imbibing spirits."

"Pray he doesn't," Meredith said grimly. Walking to the top of the steps, she started waving at the carriage as it pulled to a halt.

Holding her breath, she watched Hamilton climb out. The carriage obstructed his view of the driveway, and she prayed he wouldn't hear the clip-clop of the constable's horse, still quite a distance away.

"How nice to see you!" she cried out, as he mounted the steps, his astonished gaze on her face.

"My goodness, you certainly seem pleased to see me." He took off his hat and swept a slight bow. "To what do I owe this unexpected honor?"

She backed into the hallway and he followed her. Glimpsing the wagon approaching, she frantically signaled to Felicity with her eyes.

Felicity hastily slammed the door shut, making Hamilton turn his head in surprise. "A welcoming committee. How very flattering."

Essie uttered a small whimper, and Felicity took hold of her arm. "We were about to leave for the village," she said shortly. "We're just waiting for the carriage to arrive."

"They are going to watch the maypole dancing," Meredith said, wincing as the sound of a horse's hooves could now plainly be heard. "That must be their carriage now. Won't you please come to my office? I'll ring for Mrs. Wilkins and have her send up a tea tray."

Hamilton seemed a little bemused when he answered her. "Pardon? Oh, yes. I mean, no, thank you. Actually I came to ask you if you would . . ." His voice trailed off when he noticed both Essie and Felicity staring at him, one with fear and the other with ill-concealed impatience. "Ah . . . perhaps we should retire to your office after all. I can present my request there."

"Good." Hearing a door slam outside, Meredith turned and hurried across the lobby to the hallway. "I'll ring for Mrs. Wilkins."

"Oh, please don't bother with the tea tray." Hamilton was forced to call out after her since she was now practically running down the hallway.

The front door bell jangled as someone tugged on it. Meredith raised her voice and beckoned with her arm. "Come, Mr. Hamilton. I really can't wait to hear what you want to ask of me."

"Obviously." Looking more perplexed than ever, Hamilton followed her into the office.

With a huge sigh of relief, Meredith hastily closed the door, then rushed over to her desk to sit down before her knees gave out on her.

Hamilton flipped his coattails and sat down opposite her.

"Something has happened to you, Meredith. You have never looked so eager to talk to me. May I ask what has brought about this rather intriguing transformation?"

Now she felt foolish. What on earth could she possibly say that would explain her outrageous behavior? She had practically lured the man into her office, and now here he was, sitting with an infuriating smug look on his face, just waiting for her to enlighten him.

Staring into his eyes, she had an uneasy feeling that this time she may have gone a little too far.

Chapter 17

Searching desperately for words, Meredith decided the only option open to her was to feign ignorance. "Transformation?" Her voice came out a little too high and she made a supreme effort to lower it. "I'm not quite sure I know exactly what you mean."

Hamilton's expression turned incredulous. "Oh, come now, Meredith. Surely you're not going to deny that your welcome was a great deal more exuberant than usual? I'd just like to know why, that's all. Not that it displeases me, of course. Quite the contrary."

Meredith forced a laugh. "Exuberant? Oh, that must be because of the weather. It's such a beautiful day out there. Lovely warm sunshine and absolutely no clouds in the sky. Summer can't be too far away. I do love the summer, don't you?"

Aware that she was prattling, she pretended to cough and covered her mouth with her hand.

Hamilton frowned. "If I didn't know better, I'd think you had been keeping company with a bottle of gin."

At his mention of spirits, guilt made Meredith hiccup. She had, after all, enjoyed a large glass of cider midday, which had given her a very pleasant glow for a while.

It was the thought of the inebriated students, however, that gave her the most concern. She could only hope that Felicity would be able to hold their noise down until she could get rid of Stuart Hamilton.

"And you would be quite wrong," she assured him. "Now, what was it you wanted to ask me? If it's about the students, I'm sure they are still confined to their rooms, as you ordered." *At least most of them,* she amended silently.

Hamilton continued to stare at her for another moment or two, until she became quite uncomfortable. Then he said abruptly, "This has nothing whatsoever to do with the students. I was going to ask you the last time I was here, and somehow I got sidetracked."

Thinking back to their last conversation, and the manner in which he had left, Meredith could quite understand why he had forgotten to ask her whatever it was he wanted. She waited, in tense silence, for his next words.

"I . . . ah . . . was going to invite you to come with me to the May Day festivities. We might be a little too late now to watch the dancing on the green, but I have been asked to present the trophy to the winning dance group at the May Day ball this evening, and I would like it very much if you would consent to accompany me as my guest."

Meredith stared at him in stunned silence.

After an uncomfortable pause, Hamilton, who seemed unusually ill at ease, added, "I realize this is short notice and I deeply apologize for that, but I thought, perhaps, if I returned for you at six o'clock, that would . . . ah . . . give you time to prepare yourself for the evening. I . . . ah . . . understand there will be refreshments served, and . . . ah . . . if you were so inclined, we could dine afterward."

Meredith swallowed. "Dine?" It seemed to be the only word she could form.

"Ah, yes." Hamilton ran a finger around the inside of his collar. "At my house. I have an excellent cook, and I think you would enjoy whatever she prepares."

Alone with him in his house? No, no, she couldn't. Fighting a sense of panic, Meredith sought for a polite way to decline the unexpected invitation. She had never seen Hamilton this way. He was always so supremely confident and in control. This was a new side to him, and it made her even more uncomfortable in his presence. "That's most kind of you, Mr. Hamilton—"

"Now, Meredith. I thought we agreed that you would call me Stuart."

That sounded a lot more like the Stuart she knew. Taking a deep breath, she murmured, "Stuart, then. As I was saying, it's most kind of you to think of me, and I appreciate the kind invitation, but I couldn't possibly—"

"Don't say no just yet."

She closed her mouth and waited.

"I realize that sometimes we differ in our opinions on how the business of Bellehaven should be run, and I admit that at times, I can be a trifle stubborn."

She raised her eyebrows at this, but allowed him to continue.

"I do, however, feel that in all other matters, we share a pleasant affinity in most subjects, and I would very much like the opportunity to explore that in further detail."

Again she hesitated, but before she could voice her doubts he added, "It could be a most pleasurable evening, Meredith. Just two friends enjoying a spot of dancing and then relaxing over supper, exchanging views on worldly affairs and such. I do hope you will consent to join me."

When he looked at her with such warmth and yearning she found it difficult to deny him anything. For a second or two she actually considered accepting the unexpected invitation, but then panic set in once more.

It had been years since she had attended anything more stimulating than a choral recital at the village hall. The May Day ball was to be held in Witcheston, at the country club, and was a posh affair. There was absolutely nothing she had to wear that would be in the least suitable.

Besides, the thought of dining alone with Stuart Hamilton in his home was far too threatening to her peace of mind. "I'm so sorry," she said abruptly, "but I'm afraid I have some urgent business that needs attention. I have to prepare my classes for next week, and I—"

"It's all right, Meredith. I understand." Hamilton stood, his smile obviously forced. "As I said, it was very short notice. Perhaps another time."

"That would be very nice. Thank you." She rose to her feet, and he held out his hand. Offering hers, she felt a fluttering in her stomach as he took her fingers and drew them to his lips.

"Until later then, Meredith."

She was far too breathless to answer with anything other than a nod.

He had almost reached the door when he paused, and looked back at her. "Oh, I almost forgot. About Pratt. I managed to track down his birth date. It turns out he's not my nephew after all."

Sensing his disappointment, she said quickly, "Oh, Stuart. I'm so sorry. I know you were hoping that he would be your sister's child."

Hamilton shrugged. "Not really. Bit of a scoundrel that young chap. It's better this way." He touched his fingers to his forehead in farewell. "Until next time."

It was only after the door had closed behind him that she was able to enjoy a full breath again.

"Oh, stop sniveling, Grace." Olivia threw a petticoat into her battered suitcase. "It's not the end of the world. It's not like anybody died."

"I might as well have died." Grace sank onto her bed and sobbed. "What am I going to do?"

"You can come and stay with me and me mum until you find something else." Olivia tucked a pair of drawers into the side of the suitcase. "She won't mind. She's all right, me mum. She'll take care of you."

"But your mum lives in *London*!" Grace wailed louder.

"Crikey, Grace, it's not that bad. I grew up there, didn't I? It's not the country, I know, but there's a park nearby and lots of stuff to do."

"I don't want to live near a park and do stuff. I want to stay here."

"Well, you can't, can you. Old Moaning Minnie up there gave us the sack and good riddance to her, that's what I say."

Grace clutched her favorite afternoon frock to her chest and rocked back and forth on the bed. "It's all your fault. I told you what would happen and now it has. I'll end up in the workhouse, I know I will. I'll d-die in there." Sheer fright had her in an ugly grip now, and all she wanted to do was crawl into bed, pull the covers over her head, and pretend that all of this was a nightmare.

"Don't be silly." Olivia sat down next to her and put an awkward arm around her shoulders. "Me mum won't let you go to the workhouse. Besides, I know what happened was my fault and when I tell me mum about everything I know she'll want you to stay with us."

"What about your dad?" Grace sniffed, and drew the sleeve of her frock across her nose. "Won't he mind?"

"Me dad's dead," Olivia said, her voice short. "I told you that, remember? There's only me mum and me brother. You'll like Danny. He's a bookie."

Grace sniffed again. "What's a bookie?"

"A bookmaker, silly."

"He makes books?"

Olivia grinned. "Nah, he takes bets. You know, at the horse races."

Grace opened her mouth in surprise. "Go on!"

Olivia nodded. "Makes good money, he does. Enough to keep me mum comfortable in a small house, anyway. I tell you, Grace, it will be all right. We'll work things out somehow. We'll both get new jobs, you'll see."

Grace nodded, and got up to finish her packing. She wished she could believe Olivia, she really did, but she just couldn't stop worrying. She couldn't stay with Olivia's mum forever. She'd have to move out sooner or later, and then there'd she be, stuck in London, all on her own.

Fighting back the tears, Grace reached into the wardrobe for her nightgown. Her life was over. She just knew it.

* * *

A glance at the clock warned Meredith to make haste. The students would most likely be waiting for her in the library, and she had much to do before she could prepare for the evening.

Arriving at the library door, she heard voices raised. She threw open the door, and briefly closed her eyes. Students were sprawled in chairs, some were actually sitting on the floor. Sophie Westchester and a young girl with flaming red hair argued with Felicity, while Essie hovered anxiously nearby.

Meredith had to raise her own voice to be heard. "What on earth is going on here?"

Felicity threw up her hands in disgust. "You talk to this little brat. I've had enough of her."

Sophie turned a sulky face toward Meredith. "She won't *listen* to me!"

Meredith stepped forward. "And to whom, may I ask, are you referring as *she*?"

Sophie's face darkened. "I mean Miss Cross. She won't listen to a word I say."

Meredith looked around at the rest of the students, some of whom appeared about ready to fall asleep. "Get up, all of you. On your feet."

Groaning and muttering, the girls climbed to their feet. Meredith waited until every one of them stood in front of her before adding, "I hope you all realize the disgrace you have brought upon this school and every one of our pupils. You represent the entire school when out in public, and I dread to think what kind of impression you have left behind."

"But—" Sophie began, and Meredith cut her off with her hand.

"You will all remain in detention for the next four

weeks. No one will be allowed anywhere off the premises until after that time."

Groans and mutters of protest greeted this statement. Ignoring them, Meredith continued, "Furthermore, should any of you disobey this order again, you will be expelled immediately and sent home."

Again Sophie spoke up. "But Mrs. Llewellyn, it—"

Meredith silenced her again with a swift gesture of her hand. "I don't want to listen to any excuses, Sophie. I strongly suspect that you were the leader in this disgraceful escapade, and quite honestly I am wondering why I shouldn't expel you this very minute. If I were you, I'd keep a still tongue, and be thankful that you have escaped my wrath. Now get back to your rooms, all of you, and remain there until I give you permission to leave."

The girls filed out of the door, some of them stumbling, all of them with mutinous frowns, and as they trudged down the hallway Sophie's voice rose in protest. "But it wasn't our *fault!*"

"It never is," Felicity muttered, throwing herself down on a chair. "There's some consolation in the thought that some of those girls will have wicked headaches in the morning."

"How did they find out about the dart match, I wonder?" Meredith shook her head. "Someone must have told them. They must have known they wouldn't be allowed to stay in the public bar. Whatever were they thinking?"

Felicity sniffed. "I should have known when I first smelled the smoke in the dining room that something was afoot. Especially when I realized the fire was completely harmless. Girls that age don't think. They just act and to hell with the consequences."

Essie uttered a protesting gasp and Felicity sighed. "I beg your pardon. Excuse my swearing. I didn't mean to offend."

"Well, thank heavens Mr. Hamilton didn't see them." Meredith wandered to the window and looked out onto the sunlit lawns. "I have enough problems to cope with right now, without our illustrious owner weighing in with his biased opinions."

"Considering we are a building full of women," Felicity observed dryly, "you do seem to have a great deal of conflict with men. What with Roger Platt, Stuart Hamilton, and Lord James Stalham, you have your hands full, I'd say."

"Drat James and his problems." Meredith hugged her arms to comfort herself. "Who chose me to be a champion of lost ghosts, anyway? It wasn't something I volunteered to do, for heaven's sake. All this running around investigating takes a huge toll on my duties as headmistress, and I'm becoming quite tired of the extra work and responsibilities thrust upon me."

"I don't blame you," Essie said, her tone soothing. "It must be so worrying, trying to satisfy a ghost. It could even be dangerous. I don't know why you do it, Meredith. I really don't."

"It's all for naught, anyway. I'm no closer to finding out who killed Lord Stalham. For all I know, James could well be the killer and is simply using me to vent his anger at being denied wherever it is he wants to go."

"If the alternative is to go down below," Felicity murmured, "I really can't blame him for trying to reach a more acceptable destination."

"Well, he just might have to find his way on his own. I am at a point where I can go no farther."

A tap on the door turned Meredith's head and brought Felicity to her feet.

"What's the matter now?" she muttered, as she strode over to the door.

Mrs. Wilkins entered the room in a rush. "I'm so sorry to disturb you, ladies. The students told me you were all in here. I wouldn't have bothered you, but—"

"It's quite all right, Mrs. Wilkins." Meredith came forward to meet her. "Is something wrong?"

The cook's face crumpled, and Meredith was afraid the woman was going to burst into tears. "It's the maids, m'm. Miss Fingle's given both of them the sack. They're downstairs packing their things right now."

Meredith sighed. "What did they do now?"

Mrs. Wilkins looked up at her in surprise. "You don't know? They were the ones that started all that commotion in the Dog and Duck. At least, Olivia was. I think Grace just went along because Olivia told her to go. I don't know why that girl listens to her, that I don't."

Meredith frowned. "The maids? I didn't see them in the police station when the students were released. They went to the village with them? That's rather odd, isn't it?"

"They didn't exactly go along *with* them, m'm. They was the ringleaders, so to speak. They were the ones that started the fire in the dining room so they could all slip out in the commotion. The students followed *them*."

"That's even more strange. Why on earth would Olivia and Grace invite students to go with them to a dart match?"

It was the cook's turn to look bewildered. "Dart match? I don't know nothing about a dart match, m'm. Olivia and Grace led the students down to the pub to hold a protest.

You know, the suffragette thing. Votes for women and all that. From what I heard, it was Olivia that started smashing the glasses. The students were just having a good time with the lads down there. The barman rang for the constable and he took everyone down to the police station."

Meredith grimaced. "He would. P.C. Shipham is always ecstatic when he has an opportunity to pronounce that a finishing school for young ladies is a complete and utter waste of time and money."

"Thank heavens you heard about it, Mrs. Lewellyn," Mrs. Wilkins said, wiping her nose with a large handkerchief. "They might all still be locked up in that awful place if you hadn't gone down there."

"Actually it was Miss Pickard who heard about it first," Meredith pointed out.

Essie nodded. "Miss Cross and I were waiting for Mrs. Llewellyn to arrive and we overheard some men on the green saying there had been a commotion in the Dog and Duck. They said a crowd of young women had been arrested. We didn't take too much notice until one of them mentioned that he thought the women came from Bellehaven."

The housekeeper nodded. "Lucky for them you went down there, Mrs. Llewellyn. You must have had a devil of a time getting them all released."

Meredith smiled. "To be honest, I think P.C. Shipham was glad to be rid of them. They were making so much noise you couldn't hear yourself speak."

"Well, I'm just sorry my maids caused so much trouble."

Mrs. Wilkins lifted the corner of her apron and dabbed at her eyes. "Mrs. Llewellyn, please. Those girls are like my own daughters, they are. I don't know what I'd do without them. They're good girls, when they're not trying to act like saviors of the world, that is. They mean well, but they just seem to attract trouble. Can't you please ask Miss Fingle to reconsider? Perhaps punish them in some other way?"

Meredith sighed. "I don't like to interfere in the domestic issues, Mrs. Wilkins. That's Miss Fingle's job and she does it very well."

A tear made its way down the cook's cheek. "I know, m'm, but it's so hard to find help these days. I can't manage everything on my own."

"Oh, come on, Meredith." Felicity sat down on her chair and crossed her ankles. "After all, the maids were only trying to help the cause. They may have gone about it the wrong way, but no real harm was done. Let's pay for the broken glasses out of the budget funds and tell Miss Fingle we can't find replacements for Olivia and Grace. Which is the truth. Any female over fourteen is either married or has left the village to work in London."

"Please, Meredith?" Essie leaned forward, her forehead creased in concern. "We can't lose Olivia and Grace. We just can't."

"Very well." Meredith lifted a finger and shook it at the cook. "I'll speak to Miss Fingle. You will be responsible, however, for keeping those girls out of trouble in future. You will have to be firm with them, and make sure they understand the consequences if they disregard your orders. I might be able to persuade Miss Fingle to be lenient, but I will not interfere a second time. Is that clear, Mrs. Wilkins?"

"Quite clear, Mrs. Llewellyn." The cook smiled tearfully at her. "Thank you, m'm. I'm ever so grateful, I am."

Meredith waited for the door to close behind her, then let out her breath on a grunt of disgust. "I detest having to go against Miss Fingle's wishes."

"I don't blame you." Felicity got to her feet again. "She's a formidable old bat, but ultimately you are in charge and she will have to abide by your ruling."

"She won't be too pleased about it."

"She'll come around." Felicity glanced at the clock on the mantelpiece. "I'm going to retire to my room until supper. I have some work to catch up on."

"Me, too." Essie jumped to her feet.

Following them out into the hallway, Meredith felt suddenly weary. A quiet evening in her room would have been wonderful. But first she had to tackle Miss Fingle— something she was not looking forward to at all.

Chapter 18

When Meredith entered Miss Fingle's office a few moments later, the housekeeper dropped her pen and pushed her glasses higher up her bony nose. "Mrs. Llewellyn! I thought you were still in the village."

"No, I returned here as soon as I heard about the problem with the students."

Miss Fingle's sharp eyes glowed with anger. "Those two wretched maids have gone too far. I'll be glad to be rid of them."

"That's why I'm here." Without being invited, Meredith took a seat in front of the desk. "I think we should reconsider sacking them."

The housekeeper shot up on her chair. "I beg your pardon? You surely jest? Those girls have brought nothing but disgrace and ridicule down on this school. What Mr. Hamilton will say when he hears of this I shudder to think."

Meredith winced. "I was rather hoping we wouldn't

have to bother Mr. Hamilton with this." Borrowing Felicity's words, she added, "After all, no real harm was done."

"No harm?" Miss Fingle's harsh voice rose a notch. "No *harm*? Do you have any idea the uproar their little prank caused? To say nothing of the damage wrought upon the public house." She twisted her nose. "Not that I have any regard for such an establishment. In my opinion, public houses are nothing more than dens of iniquity, providing liquid evil that befuddles men's minds and turns them into drunken beasts."

Casting her mind back to the glass of cider she'd enjoyed in the outside garden of the Pig and Whistle in Witcheston, Meredith cleared her throat. Her choice might not have been the strong ale that the men usually consumed, but it had carried quite a punch, all the same. "I am perfectly willing to reimburse the Dog and Duck for the damage they sustained, which I believe was no more than a few glasses."

Miss Fingle pinched her lips together. "That's for Mr. Hamilton to decide."

"No," Meredith said firmly. "That is my decision. I see no reason to involve Mr. Hamilton in this matter. This is a domestic issue, and as such, shall be resolved by us. I hope you are in agreement."

For a moment the housekeeper looked as if she would protest, but then she gave a reluctant nod. "Very well. I will contact the publican"—she shuddered before continuing—"and ask for a total amount of the damage."

Meredith let out her breath. "As for the maids, I don't think I have to remind you how difficult it is to find good help these days."

Miss Fingle snorted. "That's obvious, judging by the caliber of our present servants."

"Olivia and Grace have been with us since they were fourteen," Meredith said quietly. "For the most part they have been reliable and trustworthy. Everyone makes mistakes."

Miss Fingle narrowed her eyes. "This, in my considered opinion, is one mistake too many. With all due respect, Mrs. Llewellyn, you do not deal with them on a day-to-day basis. I find them both, but especially Olivia, to be insubordinate to an extreme. I am quite sure that we would be making a grave mistake by keeping them employed in this establishment."

"Nevertheless, I feel that we would be better off with the devil we know." Meredith rose to her feet, signaling an end to the discussion. "I'm quite confident that you will find a way to control their behavior in the future. Give them whatever punishment you deem fit, but we will continue to employ them. Thank you, Miss Fingle." Leaving the outraged housekeeper sitting there open-mouthed, Meredith quickly made her escape into the corridor.

Well, she thought, as she made her way back to the room, that didn't go quite the way she had envisioned, but she had achieved her purpose, though not without raising the housekeeper's ire.

She wouldn't want to be in the maids' shoes for the next few days, but perhaps some stern treatment would temper their enthusiasm for getting into hot water.

All that evening, while working in her office, Meredith tried not to think about Stuart Hamilton dancing at the May Day ball. In spite of her good intentions, every now and then her mind wandered, and she imagined herself dressed in an elegant gown, floating across the floor, her hand clasped in his.

When the images became too frequent, and much too

vivid for comfort, she decided to retire early. It had been an exhausting day, and something told her that James would once more be disturbing her sleep.

She made her decision while preparing for bed. The very next time the ghost appeared, she would tell him she had failed in her attempts to clear his name.

Failure did not sit well with her, but she saw no other course of action. To continue would not only be fruitless, it would be disruptive, and she could no longer afford that kind of intrusion into her life.

If she had been paying more attention to what was going on around her, the incident in the Dog and Duck might have been avoided. From now on, she would attend to her duties, and James would simply have to find another way to redeem himself.

She had barely fallen asleep before waking again to a chilly room. At first she thought something else must have awakened her, since the room remained dark and still. Since she had trouble falling asleep, however, she reached for her lamp, intending to read a few pages of her Sherlock Holmes novel in the hopes of relaxing her mind.

With the faint glow of the lamp falling across the bed, she opened the book. Moments later she felt, rather than saw a presence in the room. She looked up, braced for the confrontation. The pink cloud hovered nearby, the figure of James quite clear in the center.

"I'm glad you came." Meredith set the book down and pulled the covers up to her chin. She felt somewhat vulnerable talking to a man while sitting up in bed. Even if he was dead.

James gestured with his hand, and she guessed he was asking a question.

"No," she said, "I did not discover who killed your father. I thought at first Pauline Suchier had killed him, but it seems she left before your father was shot. I also thought it might have been your mother—"

She caught her breath as the mist turned dark red and James's furious face glared back at her. "I know, I know. I just can't bring myself to believe she would let you die for a crime she committed."

Meredith waited until the mist had turned pink again before adding, "So, if you aren't the culprit, I can't imagine who the killer can be. I'm sorry. I can't help you anymore. I've done the best I can. I'm not very good at this detecting work, as you can see. Besides, I have my own work to do and I can't waste any more time on wild goose chases."

She watched the mist turn red again, reminding herself over and over that a ghost couldn't hurt her. It shocked her, however, when James lifted his hand, pointed a finger at her as if he held a gun and crooked his finger around an imaginary trigger.

He had vanished before she had fully recovered. How immature of him. Surely he must know the gesture was highly inappropriate, given the nature of his father's death. What was he trying to convey, for heaven's sake? That she had disappointed him? That she was ineffective? All true, of course, but she had done her best.

Just the idea of him pointing a gun at her, even if it wasn't real, chilled her to the bone. She could understand how Winnie must have felt, when Lord Stalham's visitor had pointed the gun at her.

Still shivering, Meredith lay down, reluctant yet to turn down the lamp. Instead, she mulled over her last thought.

Lord Stalham's visitor. With a gasp she shot up in the bed again.

Of course. How very obtuse of her. That was it. That was what she had tried to remember. Winnie telling her how the visitor had taken the gun from the cabinet the day before Lord Stalham was shot.

Concentrating now, she went over everything that she'd learned at the estate. Now that she could see it all clearly, she couldn't imagine how she had been so oblivious to the obvious. For now, without a doubt, she knew who had killed Lord Stalham.

Meredith awoke early the next morning, filled with determination. She didn't know if James would return after her outburst the night before, but nevertheless, she intended to see that his name was cleared and that the real killer paid for the crime.

"I am going to pay a visit to the Stalham estate," she told Felicity and Essie, as they sat in the teacher's lounge after having attended church. "I'd very much like you both to come along."

Both women stared at her in surprise. "I thought you'd given up on all that," Felicity said, her teacup held in the air. "Didn't you tell us yesterday that you had reached an impasse in your investigation and could go no further?"

"I did." Meredith reached for her cup and sipped the hot tea, letting it soothe her uneasy stomach. "However, I finally worked out who really killed Lord Stalham, and I need to set the record straight. Not just for James's sake, but for the sake of justice. The culprit must pay for the crime."

"You know who killed Lord Stalham?" Essie's eyes were wide as she stared at Meredith. "You mean that James didn't kill his father after all?"

"That's exactly what I mean."

"So who is it?" Essie demanded. "Do tell us."

"I'd rather not at this point." Meredith replaced her cup in its saucer. "It will make things a lot simpler if you don't know that for now. I don't want the killer to realize I know the truth until the proper moment."

Felicity frowned. "Don't tell us you are actually going to confront the murderer."

"I am." Meredith smiled. "Which is why I want both of you to come with me. I need your help."

"Don't you think"—Felicity leaned forward to accentuate her words—"that it would be wiser and a good deal safer to tell Inspector Dawson what you know and let him handle it?"

"Definitely," Meredith agreed. "But the inspector can't investigate further without solid evidence, and unfortunately, there is none. I need to get that evidence so he can arrest the right person."

Felicity rolled her eyes, while Essie looked frightened. "I hope you don't want me to talk to that awful butler again." She gasped. "Is he the killer? Oh, I just know he is."

"I promise you will both know everything just as soon as I feel I can tell you." Meredith looked from one to the other. "For now, however, all I can do is ask you to trust me."

Essie still looked as if she would rather climb a mountain on her knees than do any such thing. Felicity, on the other hand, nodded. "I just hope this is all worth the risk."

Meredith put her cup and saucer back on the tray and stood.

"My sentiments exactly. In any case, it's time to find out. Reggie is most likely waiting outside for us, so if you ladies are ready, I'd like us to be on our way."

"What exactly do you want us to do?" Felicity followed her to the door. "I hope it's not anything too strenuous. Thank heavens it's Sunday. At least we won't have to account for our whereabouts. I trust Sylvia will be able to manage, seeing that the students are still confined to their rooms."

"I certainly hope she keeps a better eye on them than she did yesterday." Meredith stepped outside and glanced down the corridor to make sure there were no stray students wandering about. "I had a word with her as we were leaving the church this morning. She seemed willing enough to watch over everything until we return. To put it in her words, she had nothing better to do with her time. Though if you ask me, she's anxious to make up for her incompetence yesterday and wants another chance to prove her worth."

"I just hope I don't have to talk to the butler," Essie said, joining them in the hallway.

"You might have to, I'm afraid." Meredith led the way to the front door. "He has forbidden me to come back to the estate, so if we manage to get inside the mansion I might need you to keep him occupied long enough for me to carry out my plan. Also, we will have to find another way into the building. We can't go through the front door and I'd rather avoid bumping into Mrs. Parker. I have a feeling she's not about to let me in the house, either." She glanced back at Felicity. "I might have to make use of your skills at opening locks."

Felicity grimaced. "At least my spell in jail taught me something useful."

Essie shuddered. "I still can't believe they put you in that awful prison simply for protesting."

"I'm afraid that's where our maids will end up if they insist on fighting for women's rights." Meredith reached the front door and opened it. "Ah, there's Reggie. Come, ladies. Let us see if we can trap a murderer."

Half an hour later Reggie halted the carriage down the lane from the Stalham estate, as Meredith had ordered. "We will walk up to the mansion and go in the back entrance," she told the other two as they set off down the road.

Instead of walking up the driveway, Meredith cut through the trees, holding up her skirt so that the brambles didn't snag the fine wool. Following close behind, Essie asked nervously, "What will happen to us if we are caught trespassing?"

"Don't worry," Meredith told her, with a great deal more confidence than she felt, "I have a friend in high places who will help us if that happens."

"If you're talking about that morose Inspector Dawson," Felicity said, stomping along behind them, "I wouldn't place too much trust in his ability to protect you. After all, he has to uphold the law, and we *are* trespassing."

"He will think it justified when I hand him Lord Stalham's killer."

"How are you planning to do that?" Essie asked anxiously. "You can't just walk up to a murderer and demand he confess to the crime."

"There are other ways to get a confession." Meredith

lowered her voice. "Now be quiet. We are nearing the mansion and I don't want to be caught by the grounds-keeper before we even get inside."

She led the rest of the way in silence, and eventually emerged from the woods at the rear of the house. "We have to cross the lawn to the French windows," she said, pointing to where the glass doors were almost hidden by a trellis of vines. "If we are quick about it, we should be able to get there unseen. Felicity, you go first in case the doors are locked. Beckon to us when you have them open."

Felicity's usual confidence seemed to have deserted her. Frowning, she stared at the seemingly vast stretch of lawn between her and the doors. "Wouldn't it just be more simple to go to the front door and demand entrance? If all three of us barge our way inside, we should be able to overpower that malicious little butler."

Meredith shook her head. "For my plan to work, I have to make it look as if I have been allowed admittance to the mansion."

"I think it's time you told us what your plan is, so we can at least be prepared."

"My plan," Meredith said quietly, "is to talk to Winnie alone in the library."

Felicity raised her eyebrows. "You hope to do this without Smithers finding out?"

"Oh, I'm sure he'll find out. I'm just hoping my plan works before that happens."

"But why—"

Meredith held up her hand. "I don't have time to explain it all now. Please, Felicity, just trust me and open those doors for us."

Felicity hesitated for a few more seconds, then nodded.

"Very well. Just remember, I've already done one spell in prison. I don't relish the thought of doing another."

"You won't," Meredith assured her, praying she could keep that promise.

She drew Essie back into the trees while Felicity sprinted across the grass to the mansion. "Essie, once we are inside the library, I want you to keep a lookout for Smithers. If it seems that he will discover us, I need you to talk to him long enough to allow Felicity and me to get out of sight. Just tell him the housekeeper let you in, and that you are looking for your parasol that you left behind the last time you were here."

Essie looked confused. "I didn't have a parasol."

"Yes, well, let's hope that Smithers doesn't remember that. Whatever you do, keep him away from the library."

Essie looked about to cry. "What if I can't?"

Meredith patted her arm. "Just do your best, dear." She looked across the lawn to where Felicity stood waving frantically. "Oh, my. We had better go. Come on, Essie. Stay close behind me."

The distance across the grass was farther than she'd thought. By the time she reached Felicity she was out of breath, and Essie's cheeks burned with the exertion.

Felicity simply pointed at the doors, which stood ajar. "They weren't locked," she whispered.

Meredith nodded, then took hold of Essie's arm. Pulling her along with her, she stepped into the library. Felicity followed her, quietly closing the doors behind her.

"Now what?" Felicity whispered.

"I want you to find Winnie and send her back here to talk to me."

Felicity's eyebrows rose. "Wouldn't it be better for you to find her and talk to her wherever she's at?"

"No, I need to be in here to talk to her. I can't make her come back here with me, but if you tell her I have something of the utmost importance to say to her, I'm hoping curiosity will bring her to me."

"You hope," Felicity said grimly. "This all sounds very unpredictable."

"That's because it is." Meredith gave her a wry smile. "I didn't say the plan was perfect."

"What about me?" Essie asked. She was actually shivering, though the room was quite warm.

Feeling sorry for her, Meredith placed her arm about her friend's slim shoulders. "Keep looking out the door. If you see Smithers coming, go out to meet him. Try to lead him away from the library, perhaps suggesting he help you look for the parasol outside."

Essie's bottom lip quivered. "He won't hurt me, will he?"

"No," Meredith said, praying she was right. "You have nothing to fear from Smithers, other than his reporting our deplorable behavior to the constabulary."

That didn't seem to reassure her. Adding a few more instructions to them both, Meredith gave Essie a little push. "Go on, Essie. I have complete faith in you."

"Lord have mercy," Felicity muttered, and followed Essie to the door.

Meredith held her breath as Essie opened the door and peered outside. Pulling her head back in, she nodded at Felicity. "It's all clear."

Felicity held crossed fingers in the air for a few seconds, then disappeared into the hallway.

Meredith stayed by the windows, ready to slip through them should Smithers get past Essie's guard and enter the room. Everything depended on getting Winnie into the library without anyone seeing her.

There were still no guarantees, of course. She had no way of knowing how Winnie would react to what she had to say. She could only hope that it all worked out as she had envisioned.

Chapter 19

It seemed that hours had passed since Felicity had left the room, yet looking at the clock, Meredith could see that only twenty minutes had gone by.

Essie still leaned in the doorway, though every now and then she pulled her head in to glance at Meredith, no doubt to assure herself that her friend was still there.

After another ten minutes or so, Meredith began to worry in earnest. Had something happened to Felicity? Had she found Winnie and run into trouble persuading the girl to come to the library? Had Smithers found them both and realized what was going on? Did— Her speculation ceased abruptly as Essie withdrew her head with a gasp.

"She's coming," she whispered, her eyes wide with apprehension.

"Winnie?" Meredith moved to the center of the room.

Essie nodded.

"Quick, Essie. Out the windows."

Essie needed no second bidding. She leapt across the room, then paused at the French doors. "You will be all right?"

"Yes, yes." Meredith waved a hand at her. "Go!"

Essie opened the doors and slipped through. She had barely escaped when Winnie tapped on the door, then opened it and walked in.

"Mrs. Llewellyn. You asked to see me?"

"Yes, Winnie, I did. I wanted to ask you another question or two."

Winnie's chin rose and a look of defiance crossed her face. "I'm done answering questions."

"Not quite. I want you to tell me what really happened the night Lord Stalham died."

"I told you what happened." Winnie eyed the door. "I don't know anything else."

"Ah, but I think you do." Meredith took a step toward her. "When I first asked you about that night, you told me you heard nothing until the arrival of the constables woke you up. Then later, you said you saw Lady Clara leaving by the back stairs, which would have been before the constables arrived."

Winnie shrugged, though her expression had grown uneasy. "I forgot about Lady Clara the first time we talked. It's been a few months since it all happened. I got confused."

Meredith nodded. "So was I for the longest time. I knew that for James to be innocent, someone else must have shot Lord Stalham. Moreover, since the only fingerprints on the gun belonged to James, I thought at first that it meant the real killer wore gloves."

Winnie stared back at her, her eyes filled with fear. "What does all this have to do with me?"

Ignoring the question, Meredith continued, "At first I thought it might have been Miss Suchier who had fired the gun. She would certainly have been wearing gloves that night. Then I found out she left before the shot was fired, so that left Lady Clara, who would also have worn gloves. Especially since you said you saw and heard her here that night."

Winnie nodded. "It could have been her. Or it could have been James, like everyone said."

"It wasn't James, Winnie. For a very simple reason. You told me about the gentleman who paid a visit to Lord Stalham the day before he was killed. Sir Gerald Mackleby, I believe you said."

"That's right."

"Sir Gerald handled the gun, I believe, then Lord Stalham put it back in the case."

"Yes, he did."

"Obviously, if James's fingerprints were still on the gun, he didn't have time to clean it. Therefore, why weren't Sir Gerald's and your master's fingerprints also on the gun?"

Winnie's mouth opened and closed before muttering, "I don't know. I don't want to know. I have to go now—"

"Not yet!" Meredith's voice cut across the room and the girl froze. "You'll go when I'm finished speaking. Now, if James didn't kill his father, then it seemed feasible that Lady Clara had shot her husband. But would a mother have allowed her son to be hanged for a crime she committed? A mother such as Lady Clara, who from all accounts is a decent, respected woman who loved her son? I seriously doubt it."

Winnie shook her head. "I don't know why you are telling me all this, m'm, but I—"

"You'll find out in just a minute." Meredith moved even closer. "The problem was, I couldn't understand how someone could have shot Lord Stalham, cleaned the gun to remove the fingerprints, and escaped the room before James arrived on the scene. Then it occurred to me. I don't know why it took so long to realize it. The answer is, of course, that the killer never left at all. He hid instead, and was still in this room when James discovered the body. It was the only way he could avoid being seen."

Winnie's bottom lip began to tremble, but she made no attempt to comment.

Meredith softened her tone. "Mrs. Parker told me that when she heard the dogs barking she came down the stairs. Smithers met her at the bottom of the stairs and told her to go back to her room. At that point the constables hadn't yet arrived. Yet she saw you in the hallway."

Tears began to glisten in Winnie's eyes.

"You slipped out of the library, didn't you, Winnie, right after James and Smithers left the room. You knew how important it was to clean the gun. Mrs. Parker told me you read the newspaper. I'm guessing you read the article on how fingerprints can now be used to catch a criminal. You knew you had to remove your fingerprints. You shot Lord Stalham—"

"No!" Winnie shook her head. "No, I didn't!"

"—then cleaned the gun before hiding somewhere in the room when you heard James leave the parlor."

"How can you say such a thing? I never would have done such a dreadful thing. I couldn't."

"But you did." Meredith took a step closer to the girl. "I have the proof I need that you shot Lord Stalham that night, and I'm taking it to Inspector Dawson."

"No! They'll take my baby away!" All of the maid's former timidity vanished. Her features grew desperate, and her eyes glittered with resolve. Turning swiftly, she grabbed a gun from the cabinet. "I won't let them take the baby away from me. I won't. It's mine, and no one can take it from me."

The gun shook in Winnie's hand. Meredith stood quite still, a cold feeling of dread creeping over her as she stared at the barrel pointed directly at her chest. "Lord Stalham was the father of your baby, wasn't he," she said quietly.

Winnie gulped. "He forced himself on me, he did. When I told him I was having the baby, he told me to get out. He was going to throw me out on the street with nothing but the clothes on me back. He owed me, he did. I told him that." She started to cry, huge, tearing sobs that shook her whole body. "I told him he had to pay for his baby, so it wouldn't starve to death. He wouldn't listen."

"So you shot him."

"I didn't mean to!" Her voice rose as she struggled to contain the sobs. "I took the gun out of the cabinet to frighten him. I told him I'd shoot him if he didn't give me money to take care of the baby. He tried to take the gun from me and it went off." Again the sobs overwhelmed her.

Meredith stepped closer, and stretched out her hand for the gun.

"No!" Winnie sprang back. "No one's going to take my baby away from me. No one."

"I'm sorry, Winnie. I don't want you to lose your baby, but you let an innocent man die for something you did. You have to pay the price for that."

"I couldn't save James! I wanted to—I didn't want him to die, but I couldn't let them hang me. Who would take care of my baby?"

"I'll find a good home for your baby. Just give me the gun. You already have two deaths on your conscience." Meredith took another step toward her. "You surely don't want a third? What good will that do? Everyone will know it was you who shot me. You will lose your baby anyway. Give me the gun and I promise your baby will have a good home with someone to love and care for it."

With tears streaming down her face, Winnie waved the gun defiantly at Meredith as she took another step forward. For a moment she thought the maid would actually pull the trigger, but then Winnie collapsed, sinking to the floor with the gun cradled against her chest.

"I didn't mean to kill him," she moaned, over and over again, as Meredith gently pried the gun out of her fingers. "I didn't mean to kill him."

"I know you didn't," Meredith said softly, "but he's dead, all the same. So is his son. I hope now that James can find his way home."

"I don't understand, Meredith," Felicity said, seating herself by the fire in the teacher's lounge. "When did you realize it was Winnie who shot Lord Stalham?"

Meredith sipped her tea before answering. "It was after the last time I saw James's ghost. I remembered Winnie saying that both a visitor and Lord Stalham had handled the gun the day before he was shot. Since Smithers cleaned the gun only once a month, it occurred to me then that both his and the visitor's fingerprints would have been on the gun, as well as those of James."

Essie, seated across the room, looked confused. "I don't understand. What does that have to do with Winnie?"

Meredith smiled. "It was a matter of elimination. I realized the killer must have cleaned the gun, then, having no time to escape from the room before James arrived on the scene, hid somewhere in the room until after James and Smithers had left."

Felicity stared at her for a moment, then nodded. "Ah, I see."

"I don't." Essie leaned forward. "Tell me how you knew it was Winnie."

"Simple, really. I—"

Felicity raised her hand. "No, wait! Let me tell her. See if I got it right." Meredith nodded, and Felicity continued, "If the killer was hidden in the room, then obviously it wasn't Smithers, since he came in after James arrived. It couldn't have been Mrs. Parker, since Smithers met her at the foot of the stairs. Mrs. Parker, however, saw Winnie in the hallway, presumably outside the library door, where she'd slipped out after James and Smithers had left."

Essie still looked confused. "What about Lady Clara? Where does she fit in all this?"

"She doesn't," Meredith said. "I think once Winnie realized that I suspected James wasn't the killer, she made up the story about Lady Clara to throw suspicion off herself."

"Poor Mrs. Parker," Essie murmured. "She was so shocked to find out Winnie had killed Lord Stalham."

"As was Smithers. Neither of them had any idea it was Winnie." Felicity shook her head. "You took a terrible chance, Meredith. How did you know she wouldn't shoot you? We could have been planning your burial right now."

Essie cried out in protest. "Oh, Felicity, don't say such things. I have never been so frightened in my life, listening outside those doors to everything that was going on in the library. I was so sure she was going to shoot you, Meredith. I wanted to dash in there and rescue you."

"I'm glad you didn't." Meredith smiled at her. "I might not have pried a confession out of Winnie if you had. Besides, I was in no real danger."

"No real danger?" Felicity shook her head. "That girl is unstable and totally unpredictable. She could have shot you without really meaning to, the way she says she shot Lord Stalham."

"She would not have done me any harm."

"How can you possibly know that?"

Meredith shrugged. "There weren't any bullets in the gun."

Essie gasped, while Felicity seemed dumbfounded. "No bullets?" she said at last. "How did you know that?"

Meredith leaned back in her chair, rather enjoying the sensation she'd caused. "The first day I went to the estate, I saw Smithers and Mrs. Parker talking to Winnie at the end of the hallway. I read Mrs. Parker's lips. Apparently Winnie had told Smithers I was asking about the guns, and Mrs. Parker asked him if he'd removed all the bullets as he'd promised to do. Smithers must have said he had, since Mrs. Parker said she was glad he had taken care of it."

Essie made a strangled sound in her throat.

"You could have told us that," Felicity said crossly. "You frightened poor Essie to death."

"I'm sorry. I'm afraid I just didn't think of it at the

time. I was worried that you would not find Winnie before Smithers found me."

"Well, I wasn't too happy having to go back to the carriage and send Reggie into town to bring back the inspector." Felicity shook her head. "When I got back and Essie told me what had happened, I just . . ." Her voice trailed off as she rolled her eyes.

"Well, all's well that ends well." Meredith sighed. "I have to admit, I feel terribly sorry for Winnie. Though when I talked to Edward, he said he thought Winnie might have a chance of escaping the gallows. She didn't mean to kill Lord Stalham, she was just trying to make sure her baby would survive. It was an accident, and if she'd confessed to it right away things might have been different."

"But instead, she let James hang," Felicity said. "What will happen to her now?"

"Edward said she will certainly have to serve time in prison."

Essie uttered a choked sob. "What about the baby?"

"I don't know." Meredith sighed. "I suppose they will find a place for it in an orphanage somewhere. Perhaps, in time, if Winnie is released, she might be able to reclaim her child."

"How sad." Felicity shook her head. "It must be so hard for her to give up her baby. That's punishment enough for any woman."

Essie leapt to her feet as another sob erupted from her. Without a word she rushed to the door and disappeared.

Felicity stared at Meredith. "What on earth is the matter with her?"

Meredith hesitated. "I . . . have never told you this before," she said at last. "I probably shouldn't be telling you now, but I think it's time you knew. It will explain a lot about Essie, and it might help you understand why she is so emotional at times."

Felicity looked intrigued. "Go on."

"First, you must swear to me you won't repeat this story to anyone else."

Felicity held a hand over her heart. "I so swear."

"Also, I want to be the one to tell Essie that I told you her story. I want her to understand why I did so."

"Agreed."

"Very well." Meredith paused, trying to find the right words to begin. "Although Essie never talks of it, she comes from a highly regarded aristocratic family."

"She does? How odd. What on earth is she doing teaching in a finishing school?"

"I'm coming to that. Five years ago, when Essie was seventeen, she became involved with a married man."

Felicity raised her eyebrows. "I've always known she had a way with men, but I would have thought she had more sense than that."

Meredith made a face. "Who has sense at seventeen?"

"Granted." Felicity settled back. "Go on."

"Well, unfortunately, Essie found out she was expecting a baby. In order to hide the shame and disgrace from her family, she sought help to rid herself of it. It was the wrong kind of help, and although she succeeded in losing the child, she almost died herself."

Felicity's face was now full of sympathy. "Poor child. What a terrible ordeal to go through."

"When she recovered, her father strongly suggested that she find a line of work, since no man would want her now that she had disgraced herself and her family. I was looking for a tutor at the time, and Essie's background made her a perfect choice to teach the finer points of etiquette and social behavior."

Felicity nodded. "Having learned that cruel a lesson at such a young age, she would certainly be able to give others advice."

"Precisely. Anyway, I felt you should know. Sometimes you are a little impatient with her. This might help you to be a little more tolerant."

Felicity's mouth twisted in a wry smile. "I am what I am, Meredith. I'll always speak my mind. Which brings me to a point. Since when did you call our illustrious chief inspector, Edward?"

Meredith smiled. "Just recently."

"My, oh my. First Stuart and now Edward. Where will it all end?"

Meredith laughed out loud. "I have no idea, but it does make life interesting."

Felicity nodded in agreement. "It does indeed."

"Anyway, I hope that Winnie has learned a lesson, too. I hope she survives her punishment, and comes out of prison a better person. Most of all, I hope she can be reunited with her child." Meredith's eyes misted over. "I know what it's like to lose a baby. So does Essie. I hope Winnie doesn't have to lose hers."

"Amen. What about James? Do you think he can pass on now?"

"I certainly hope so. More than that, I hope he is the last ghost I'll ever see. I'm just not astute enough for this type of work. I'd much rather leave all that to people like Edward."

Felicity laughed. "Maybe you should join forces with him. You'd make quite a pair."

Her cheeks warming, Meredith shook her head. "Thank you, Felicity dear, but I'm quite happy being the headmistress of Bellehaven. That's quite enough adventure for me." She picked up her teacup, and uttered a gentle sigh of contentment.

*E*nter the rich world of
historical romance
with Berkley Books.

Lynn Kurland

Patricia Potter

Betina Krahn

Jodi Thomas

Anne Gracie

Love is timeless.
penguin.com